"I didn't plan

As if that made any d

He began to pace. Fi

"What do you want? I .... you say."

He was in love with someone else. What did he expect her to say?

"Leave." She closed the dishwasher door, unable to bear looking at him. He was a liar, a traitor. Maybe he'd never even loved her. "The sooner, the better."

"And tonight?"

"I don't care where you stay. Just not here."

"Are you sure?"

What a question. She wasn't sure of anything anymore. How could she be, after what he'd just told her?

She went into the laundry room. While she was there she heard the electric garage door open. When she came out, he was gone.

She sank onto a chair by the phone she'd used only twenty minutes earlier and glanced at the wall calendar nearby. With shaking hands she flipped through the months. June, July, August, September, October, November, December. With one of the girls' washable markers she put a big cross over the twentieth.

The due date for her fourth child.

The child Kirk didn't even know she was expecting.

Dear Reader,

This summer, my husband, our two daughters and I revisited
Port Carling, Ontario, with my husband's sister and her
family. Once again, I fell under the spell of this captivating
resort town that sits at the hub of Lake Muskoka and Lake
Rosseau, just a few hours north of Toronto.

Standing on Steamboat Bay—a wooden dock lined with
boutiques on either side—I looked out over the turquoise
waters of Indian River, which connects the two lakes, and
thought of the families that have summered here generation
after generation. I imagined traditions like the bonfire and
wiener roast that Claire Ridgeway and her family host to
mark the beginning of the season. I imagined hot summer
nights spent sipping wine on a dock and hotter days in the
lake or perhaps waterskiing with friends.

Lives change: there are new schools, new jobs, new friends,
new lovers. But come summer, there is the cottage, and the
friends who return year after year. Friends like Mallory and
Drew Driscoll and their daughter, Angel; and Grady Hogan
and his twin boys, Warren and Taylor.

This particular summer, Claire Ridgeway needs those friends
and the security of her cottage more than ever before. The
impossible has happened, shattering the illusion of her
perfect little world. Now everything is at stake and she must
make the right decision for all of them.... For herself and
her husband, Kirk, for their three young daughters and for
The Fourth Child.

I hope you enjoy her story.

C.J. Carmichael

THE FOURTH CHILD
C.J. Carmichael

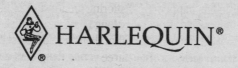

HARLEQUIN®

TORONTO • NEW YORK • LONDON
AMSTERDAM • PARIS • SYDNEY • HAMBURG
STOCKHOLM • ATHENS • TOKYO • MILAN • MADRID
PRAGUE • WARSAW • BUDAPEST • AUCKLAND

ISBN 0-373-70917-X

THE FOURTH CHILD

Copyright © 2000 by C.J. Carmichael.

Visit us at www.eHarlequin.com

Printed in U.S.A.

ACKNOWLEDGMENT

Thanks to my sister-in-law April and her husband, Paul, for many beautiful weekends at their cottage on Lake Muskoka, and for hours spent touring on *The Duke*.

DEDICATION

This story is for my family: my husband, Michael, and our daughters, Lorelle and Tessa. There are days when, like Claire, all I want to do is hold you close.

CHAPTER ONE

"LOOKS LIKE I'LL BE WORKING late again tonight."
The lie came so easily Kirk Ridgeway almost believed it himself. Hands joined behind his head for support, he leaned back in his padded leather chair and stared at a painting on the wall. He was using the speakerphone, so he had no need to hold the receiver in his hand.

"I see." The woman's faint voice echoed against the office walls. "How late?"

Kirk checked his watch. It was six o'clock Wednesday. From the open door to his office he'd been watching people leave for the past hour. Soon, the brokerage firm would be all but deserted....

"Hard to say." Into the resulting silence, he added, "Tell the kids I love them, and don't bother waiting up."

He leaned forward to disconnect the line and reassured himself he *hadn't* lied. After all, he'd promised to review that new biotech prospectus to see if any of his clients might be interested in investing. Eager to assuage his conscience, he slipped on his reading glasses and reached for the thick booklet. He flipped the pages, past the cover page describing the offering and the warning to investors about the speculative nature of the venture, to the description of the business. His gaze paused at the first black heading; his mind stalled.

What was keeping her? He was sure he'd seen all the brokers who worked at his end of the building leave. His assistant had gone over an hour ago. Already the place had the hollow, muted atmosphere he associated with afterhours and weekends.

And Janice.

His eyes shifted from the prospectus, back to the painting on the wall opposite him. An abstract he'd bought recently, it evoked passionate emotions, reminding him of how he felt when he was with her.

What the hell are you doing, man? The warning voice came from inside his own head, but Kirk didn't want to listen. His chest was tight, his breathing shallow. This was getting crazy. Six months earlier he would have said he and Janice were just friends. Their relationship had started with the occasional innocent lunch—Janice had been very upset after her divorce.

Occasional lunches became more frequent; open meetings evolved into secret rendezvous. At what point had he known he was falling in love? Kirk still wasn't sure. But he did know the time had come to do something about it. Last week at dinner, Janice had told him she wanted more. He couldn't pretend not to understand what she meant.

"Hi, there."

The sound of her voice had him sitting taller in his chair, his tension, the accompanying sliver of guilt, lessening at the sight of her. Her thin, elegant silhouette was framed seductively in the pale light from the doorway. With a warm smile she entered his office and closed, then locked, the door behind her.

"About time you got here," he said.

She was wearing a form-fitting black suit, skirt short, heels high. Her silk blouse was buttoned low. Lower, he was certain, than when he'd seen her at the coffee station earlier that afternoon.

"I thought the day would never end." She leaned back against the door, her svelte figure on perfect display.

The rules of the game were about to change, Kirk sensed, and he was filled with an ambiguous swirl of emotions. Excitement, longing, guilt and self-doubt. What was he doing? Was this really what he wanted? Could he stop if he chose to?

He stood, moved toward her, then hesitated. "I feel as if I've been waiting forever...."

"I know." Her lips shimmered with fresh red lipstick, and now he was close enough to smell her perfume. It was a warm, musky scent he found both exciting and disturbing, like that new painting on his wall.

"Have you considered what we talked about last time?" she asked.

"Oh, yeah." He brought the back of his hand to her hair and brushed it from her shoulder. Since last week's dinner, he'd thought of precious little else than her desire to make love with him.

"What about here, Kirk? What about now? The place is deserted. I've locked the door."

He groaned. God, he couldn't believe it. She was offering him his ultimate fantasy. How many nights had he lain awake thinking of something just like this? Now he swallowed, his gaze automatically settling on the hint of cleavage between the parted layers of silky blouse.

"Doesn't that sound nice?" she asked, her voice an enticing whisper. She unbuttoned her jacket, let it fall from her shoulders.

Kirk pressed fingers to his forehead, where he felt a hot, sticky film of sweat. How had they come to this point? His chest pushed against his light wool jacket as he filled his lungs with air. He couldn't think about what could happen right here, right now, if only he gave the answer she was looking for.

"Kirk?" Her jacket lay on the floor, and it was obvious she had no bra under her flimsy white blouse. He felt his pulse pounding in his throat, and someplace lower, too. An aching, desperate throbbing that made it hard to think of anything else. God, how he ached to—

"Don't you want me, Kirk?" she asked. "Why haven't you kissed me yet?"

"If I kiss you, this time I won't be able to stop there."

"But that's okay," Janice said, leaning in toward him. "That's what I've been trying to tell you."

Kirk put his hands out to her shoulders. Partly to stop her from coming closer, partly to feel the warm softness of her flesh. His gaze dipped to the outline of her nipples, the hard nubs clearly visible beneath the thin film of silk, then returned to the fullness of her lips.

Oh, God, I'm a fool. Why not just kiss her? Isn't it what we both want?

But of course it wasn't that simple. He took another deep breath and straightened his shoulders. With closed eyes, he thought of a different woman, two rings, a spoken vow.

"Let's go out for dinner, Janice. We need to talk."

CHAPTER TWO

"MOM-M-M-M!" THE WAIL TRAVELED down the stairs to the kitchen, where Claire Ridgeway had just picked up the phone to make an important call. She'd been waiting for office hours, which began at eight. Now she replaced the receiver and decided she'd been overly optimistic thinking she'd have five minutes to herself before the kids caught the bus for school.

Instead, she jogged up the stairs for about the tenth time that morning. Her eldest daughter, Andie, was standing in the middle of her room, dressed in a T-shirt and panties.

"I don't have any clean jeans."

Claire scanned the room and spotted one pair under the bed and another peeking out from a pile of stuffed animals.

"No clean jeans? I wonder why." She checked the hamper in her daughter's closet. "There aren't any in the laundry.... What a puzzle."

"Mom-m-m-m." Andie put her hands on her slim hips, obviously not amused. "What am I supposed to wear?"

"How about that pretty skirt your grandma sent you from Florida?"

Claire pressed her lips together to stop from laughing at the look of disdain her daughter gave her. Andie hadn't worn a skirt to school in years. Giggles from the bathroom distracted Claire from the jeans dilemma, and she opened the door to find her six-year-old daughter, Jenna, piling a blob of mousse onto her baby-fine hair as middle sister, Daisy, watched.

"I think you're supposed to comb it in or something," Daisy suggested.

"Oh, it's sticky." Jenna touched the dollop of mousse with one finger and it shivered like jelly.

"You're supposed to put it on when your hair is wet," Claire said. "And not nearly so much." She pulled a tissue out of the box that rested on the back of the toilet and scooped up most of the mousse.

"Now, brush your hair. The bus will be here in ten minutes."

Every morning it seemed impossible that all three girls would make it to the street corner on time, yet somehow it happened. This morning was no exception. Claire dropped kisses on clean cheeks and passed out lunch bags from the front door.

"Don't forget I'm playing at Alex's house after school," Daisy said.

"Okay. I'll pick you up at five."

Andie was the last out the door. She slipped past Claire wearing rumpled jeans with grass stains at the knees. A flash of yellow signaled the approaching bus. Claire had no time to object to Andie's attire—something her daughter had definitely counted on.

"I think I'm going to have to introduce you to the washing machine after school," Claire threatened.

"Gotta go, Mom. I'm late."

Claire blew a kiss after her, that last phrase catching in her mind. *I'm late.*

Now she could make her phone call at last.

Claire's fingers trembled as she dialed the number, and the trembling only got worse when she was put on hold.

"No, I can't wait," she muttered at the recorded music, which was probably intended to be soothing. "My life, my family's life, is at stake here."

Whitney Houston didn't seem to care. She kept singing for another two stanzas, only to be cut off in the middle of a final, piercing high note.

"We have your results, Ms. Ridgeway."

Claire listened, said goodbye, hung up the receiver. For a second she just stood there, then she reached for the family calendar that hung on the wall by the phone.

"Have the girls left for school?"

Claire started. The calendar pages slipped from her hand.

"Kirk. I thought you'd left already." Her husband was dressed for the office in his suit and tie, but a glance at the clock on the microwave confirmed he was about an hour late. Claire frowned. Kirk never slept in. In all their twelve years of marriage, she'd never seen him tardy for work.

Automatically, she moved to the cupboard where they kept the mugs. "Would you like coffee and a muffin for the ride?"

Kirk usually got his own breakfast and was out of the house by seven-thirty for his forty-five-minute commute to downtown Toronto. He left just about the time the rest of them were getting up.

"No."

His voice sounded dry. He cleared his throat and said again, "No, thanks."

She'd found the aluminum mug he normally took with him in the car. "Not even coffee? I have some made."

"That's okay."

She put the mug back and eyed her husband. He was as immaculately dressed as always, freshly shaven, the curls in his dark blond hair neatly combed down, so why did he look different?

"Are you sick?"

He sighed and sat on a stool by the counter of

the island they'd installed when they'd remodeled their kitchen three years ago.

Something warned her this was serious, and Claire put a hand to her stomach, which was suddenly flipping like the pancakes she'd made for the girls that morning.

"What's wrong?" Could he have lost his job? He'd seemed distracted lately; that was for sure. But he was the highest-grossing broker at the office....

Or had he guessed? She took a deep breath, ready to defend herself.

"There's something I've been meaning to talk to you about," Kirk said. "And I didn't want the girls around."

"Oh?" He must have figured it out. All the usual signs were there. Not that he'd appeared to notice any of them. When was the last time they'd made love? Weeks ago, she was sure.

"I'm afraid I don't know where to start." Kirk was talking to her but not looking at her. And his voice was dry, as if he were nervous.

Claire was suddenly quite certain that her husband *hadn't* guessed. That he was talking about something completely unrelated to her morning telephone call.

"What's the problem, Kirk?"

He still wouldn't look at her. "I know I haven't been around much these past few months..."

No, he hadn't. Work—it was always work with Kirk. And frankly, she was getting sick of it. These days she felt as though she was raising their three daughters virtually on her own.

"I guess that hasn't been fair to you, and I'm sorry about that," he continued. "But I'm sure you'll agree that we can't always predict what life has in store for us...."

What in the world was he driving at? Afraid to interrupt, Claire leaned back against the counter, her anxiety escalating.

"What I'm trying to say is that sometimes new situations arise. Circumstances can change...."

Anxiety became dread. Claire gripped the counter behind her; whatever Kirk was trying to say, it had to be awful.

Finally, their eyes connected, the contact quick and sharp, like the plunging of a dagger.

"The thing is, Claire, I've fallen in love with someone else."

THE MOTOR from the refrigerator suddenly kicked in—the only sound in the now-still room. Claire stared at the polished hardwood floor and followed the pattern of the wood grain as it circled round and round in ever-narrowing, concentric ovals.

Air. It was gone; she couldn't breathe. Pain stabbed into her abdomen with shocking intensity.

Someone else.

Could she have heard right? Must have. Kirk's expression as he gazed at the kitchen counter was miserable. Her mind scurried to make sense of the bombshell.

In love with someone else? It couldn't be. This was Kirk. *Her* Kirk. They'd tucked in their children together last night, then shared the same bed.

A spasm of bitterness tightened her rib cage; her stomach cramped; bile rose in her throat.

She was going to be sick. But she couldn't; she had to stand here and face this. How could it have happened? The answer was painfully obvious. Kirk always worked long hours, and lately they'd been even longer than usual. Had there been other signs she'd missed? They'd been making love less frequently. And saying *I love you* even less.

There'd been a time, not that long ago, when they'd both spoken the endearment almost daily. Now she couldn't recall the last time she'd heard him say it to *her,* not the girls.

"Who is she?" Claire was amazed at how calm she sounded. In movies—because that was where stuff like this usually happened—didn't the woman start ranting and raving at this point? But she had no strength for that. Standing, choking out a few words were hard enough.

"Janice. From work."

Claire knew the name. Knew the woman. "We had her to dinner last fall."

"Yes." Kirk glanced at her, then returned his gaze to the counter.

No. She couldn't bear this. It was too awful. It was too impossible. Janice was a brokerage assistant, almost ten years younger than Claire. A fine-boned, slender young woman, with large, light brown eyes and a wide, generous smile.

"Didn't she just separate from her husband?" Claire remembered her own last-minute panic when Kirk had told her to set one less place on the table. There'd been eight of them invited from the office, until Janice's husband had canceled unexpectedly.

"They're divorced now. She went through a rough period when they decided to split. I guess that's when it all got going between us. She needed someone to talk to, and I was handy. We began going out for lunch every now and then, and..."

Claire turned her back and started unloading the dishwasher. She had to *do* something or she'd crumple to the floor or, worse yet, pound Kirk's chest.

Kirk *was* easy to talk to. Or so she remembered from the days when he'd been around enough for her to have the opportunity.

"So that's where you've been these past few months when you said you were working late." She let the salad plates drop with a clatter in the cupboard.

"Usually, I *was* working." He paused before admitting, "Sometimes we went out to dinner."

Dinner. Claire imagined candlelight and clean linens, wine and beautifully prepared entrées. While she ate at home at the kitchen table, alone with their three children.

With a violent tug, she opened the cutlery drawer and tossed in knives, forks, spoons, paying no regard to which little compartment they belonged in.

"It's not what you think," Kirk said. "We haven't been sleeping together."

She slammed the drawer. "How honorable."

"God, Claire. I was hoping we could talk rationally about this—"

"Rationally?" Claire gripped the handle of a stainless-steel knife, watching as the blood drained from her fingers. "We're not talking stock markets or investment portfolios here. You've just told me you're in love with someone else. What the hell do you expect from me?"

Kirk stood, his hands clenched by his side. "I know it's a shock. All I'm saying is we need to talk."

"It sounds like we needed to talk before you started those cozy little lunches with...Janice." To spit out the name took effort.

"Maybe."

She heard him pull in a deep breath.

"What about the kids?"

Claire straightened and glared at him. "Yes, what about the kids, Kirk? Did you ever think of them when you were having your lovely romantic evenings?"

God. Her husband was in love with another woman. This man she'd thought was her partner, her lover, her friend was really a stranger. For months he'd been lying, sneaking around behind her back...

Claire's memory flashed to their wedding day, to her vibrant happiness. To Kirk's loving hand around her, steadying her as they stood in front of the church full of people. To her, that day had been perfect, despite the rain, the mix-up about flowers, her father's rambling speech. She and Kirk had been in love. They truly had.

And now he'd fallen in love with someone else. Their marriage had ended after just twelve years. The ramifications crashed through her mind. She was going to be on her own, raising three children. Would she have to go back to work? Put the girls in after-school care? Then in seven months...

Oh, God. What was she going to do?

"I didn't plan it, Claire."

As if that made any difference.

He began to pace. Finally, he stopped in front of her. "What do you want? I'll do whatever you say."

He was in love with someone else. What did he expect her to say?

"Leave." She closed the dishwasher door, unable to bear looking at him. He was a liar, a traitor. Maybe he'd never even loved her. "The sooner the better."

"And tonight?"

"I don't care where you stay. Just not here."

"Are you sure?"

What a question. She wasn't sure of anything anymore. How could she be, after what he'd just told her? Claire kept her face averted as she picked up the roast she'd taken out to thaw earlier.

Thursday was one of the few nights that the girls were free. No dance classes, no soccer. She'd planned on making a nice meal and phoning Kirk at work to see if he could come home in time to eat with them. Then later, perhaps they'd all watch a video together.

She went into the laundry room to return the roast to the freezer. While she was there she heard the electric garage door open. When she came out, he was gone.

Claire sank onto the chair by the phone she'd used only twenty minutes earlier and glanced at the calendar. With shaking hands, she flipped past the months. June, July, August, September, October, November, December, January. With one of the girls' washable markers she put a big cross over the fifteenth.

The due date for her fourth child.

CLAIRE WENT TO THE BATHROOM and threw up. It wasn't morning sickness. She hadn't been nauseous during her previous pregnancies, and she was almost at her first trimester.

"Your pregnancy test came back positive," the nurse had told her. "Congratulations."

Congratulations. Ha. Ten minutes later her husband was telling her he was in love with another woman. Incredible timing.

And to think she'd felt he might have figured out she was pregnant. Obviously, his mind had been occupied with things other than his wife for quite some time now.

Or maybe he hadn't guessed because, like her, he hadn't wanted to know. Both of them had been thrilled about their first three kids, but they'd never planned on a fourth. In fact, for the past few years Kirk had been talking about getting a vasectomy.

Maybe now he wouldn't. Janice was young and she didn't have any children.

Claire splashed cold water on her face. She couldn't stand to think of Kirk remarrying, starting a new family. How would the girls feel about their father beginning a new life with someone else?

He was *their* daddy.

He was *her* husband.

Or so she'd thought.

Oh, God. Oh, God, she couldn't stand to think about that. About him and Janice...

About what life was about to become. How could this be happening to her, Claire Ridgeway, the woman who had it all? Beautiful children; a successful, handsome husband; a lovely home; a luxurious cottage in Muskoka. She belonged to the school council, volunteered at the school library and was renowned for her fabulous dinner parties.

She had never thought she defined herself in terms of her husband, but now she realized how their life together underpinned everything she did. If they separated, her life would change in almost every imaginable way. As would their children's.

She thought about the way the girls always came running when they heard Kirk enter through the garage. "Daddy's home! Daddy's home!"

Would she ever hear those words again?

Would they even be able to afford to stay in the same house? Maybe she'd have to move with the kids to a condo.

She needed a lawyer. Buddy Conroy, an old friend from Port Carling, jumped to mind. He'd gone into semiretirement this year, but surely he'd handle this case for her. They'd known each other forever; he was practically family.

Divorce. Funny how she'd never felt it could

happen to her. Now that it was staring her in the face, she wondered why she hadn't seen it coming.

Claire thought about the people they would have to tell. Kirk's mother, in the nursing home just a few miles from their house. Her own parents, who'd retired to Florida last year. All their family, all their friends...

Oh, God. Oh, God...

At least the school year was ending next week. They'd have the summer to sort through everything. If the children had to change schools, they'd be able to start fresh in September.

"Marriages fall apart every day," she told her reflection. "Other women live through it. So will you."

But how?

Claire moved closer to the mirror and stared into her eyes, eyes that Kirk claimed were the color of the irises that bloomed every spring under their front window. Who was this woman staring back at her?

A wife. A mother. Who else? What did other people see? What did they think?

Claire blinked and tried to be realistic. Maybe she looked good for a woman in her late thirties, but there was no question she'd left her twenties behind. For years she'd been relying on her hairdresser to maintain the pale yellow hair color of her youth. And her body...

Claire smoothed the cotton shirt that lay over her belly, already feeling the swelling that was her baby. And Kirk hadn't even noticed....

Maybe he'd thought she was just gaining more weight. She'd never lost those last five pounds after Jenna....

Squaring her shoulders, she straightened. She caught her reflection in the mirror again. Not much change from the image she'd seen that morning while she'd brushed her teeth and washed her face, following the same pattern as every other morning, getting herself dressed before she woke the girls to ready them for school.

Yes, she looked the same, but inside she felt like a completely different person. With one sentence, her world had shifted.

Whatever happened, it would never be the same again.

CHAPTER THREE

"Mommy, where's my brush?"

"Do I *have* to have a bath?"

"Did I tell you my science project is due tomorrow?"

Claire checked her watch, and her temper. Soon they would be in bed, and she'd have the peace and quiet she craved. None of this was their fault, and she had to protect them as best she could. That meant acting normal, even though her entire body burned with the pain that had threatened to swamp her all day.

"I think I saw your hairbrush on the coffee table in the family room," she told Jenna. "Go get it and I'll do your hair for you."

There were four bedrooms on the second story. The master bedroom was on one side of the wide hall, which opened to the vaulted ceiling of the living room below, and the girls' bathroom and bedrooms were on the other.

Privacy was getting to be a big deal now, especially with Andie, who was ten, and Daisy, who was eight. Claire knocked at the bathroom door, then peered inside. Daisy was sitting on the floor, her head bent over a book of Archie comics.

"Yes, you must have a bath. It's Thursday, isn't it?"

Daisy looked up through a screen of curls. "But that isn't fair. Why don't Andie and Jenna have to have baths tonight?"

"Because I like them more than I like you." Claire sighed. Daisy knew that the other girls had taken their baths on Wednesday while she was at her soccer game. She was just being fractious.

"You know, when you were little, you used to love a good soak." Claire put the stopper in the tub and turned on the faucet.

"But the water will make my pages soggy."

Claire took the comic book from her daughter's hands. "You can read when you're in bed. And don't forget to wash your hair." She ran a hand over her daughter's soft blond hair. Both Daisy and Jenna shared her coloring, although Daisy had somehow ended up with natural curls, like Andie. Only, Andie's hair was red. A brilliant orange, actually. Claire and Kirk had never figured out where that had come from.

Kirk. Just thinking the name was like touching a hot iron. Even a brief second could burn.

Claire checked the water temperature, then turned off the tap. "Please remember to use conditioner,'' she added before she closed the bathroom door.

She walked down the hall to Andie's room. "Is your assignment almost done?"

"I haven't even started." Andie was lying on her bed, playing her Game Boy. Claire stood in the doorway, wondering what had happened to the straight-A student so compulsive about doing her homework the moment she came home from school.

"Don't you think you should?"

Andie didn't even glance up from her handheld electronic game. "I forgot my books at school."

"Oh, well. I'm sure that will be okay, then. It's not like this project is going to affect your final grade, is it?"

"It only counts for twenty percent," Andie explained. A series of high-pitched beeps seemed to get her excited. She moved closer to her lamp, fingers dancing along the small buttons at the bottom of the game. "Yes! I've got him!"

Claire sat at the edge of her bed. "Andie, could you turn that off? We need to talk."

"I found my brush!" Jenna came into the room, smiling, waving the brush like a trophy.

"Would you get out of here?" Andie snapped. "You didn't even knock."

Jenna's brow creased and her smile slipped away. She looked at her mother uncertainly.

"Andie, turn that game off this minute. If you've forgotten your homework, then you're not allowed to play video games. You can read, if you want. I'll be back to talk once Jenna's in bed."

Claire stood up and walked to the doorway, gazing back at her eldest daughter. Andie had changed this year. She was acting so much like a rebellious teen that it was hard to remember she was only ten.

Maybe it was the red hair.

After brushing Jenna's hair, Claire went back to the closed bathroom door.

"Daisy, are you still in the bath?"

"Yeah."

"Well, it's time to come out now."

"I don't want to."

On a better day Claire would have seen the humor. But today was definitely not one of her better days. "Get out right now, Daisy. And remember to let the water out of the tub." She hated when the kids forgot to pull the plug. Invariably, she wouldn't realize until later, when she was doing her late-night check before turning in herself. Cold water, soap scum floating on the surface... She shivered, thinking about having to insert her hand to release the plug.

Back in Jenna's room she found the six-year-old snuggled beneath her quilt.

"Will you sing to me, Mommy?"

"Of course." She'd crooned lullabies to all three girls when they were small. Funny how she couldn't remember when or why she'd stopped with the other two. But she was glad Jenna still enjoyed the ritual.

After two favorites, Claire stood up to leave.

Jenna grabbed her hand. "Mommy, when's Daddy coming home?"

"He's away for a few days," she improvised.

"On another business trip?"

Claire nodded. "You'll see him soon, sweetheart."

She backed into the hall, pain knifing her in the middle. How was she ever going to tell her children the truth?

It was all so horrible. And so completely unexpected. Kirk, in love with another woman. She never would have believed it—especially given his parents' divorce, his experiences as a child.

Back to Andie, who was reading with her old stuffed dinosaur shoved against her chest, just under her chin. Pale light shone from a lamp beside her desk, allowing Claire to make out the shapes of the postcards Andie had tacked all over her walls.

"Did you say Daddy was on a business trip?"

Lying to Andie was harder. She was older, and her ties to her father were very close. "Why do you think you forgot to bring your assignment home, hon?''

''I don't know. I just forgot.'' Andie twisted a strand of her hair and put it in her mouth.

Claire winced at the crunching sound of her daughter's teeth on the hair. ''Please don't do that, Andie. It's such a disgusting habit.''

Andie tucked her hair behind her ear, sighed and rolled over onto her back. ''Why am I the only one in the family who doesn't have blond hair? Red is such an ugly color. I hate it.''

''I promise you won't when you're older.''

Andie sighed again. ''When is Daddy coming home?''

''I'm not sure. But he won't be happy to hear you haven't been doing your homework.''

Not that this was the first time. Andie's interest in school had started to wane about the same time as her friendship with a girl named Erin had ended, shortly after Christmas. There had to be some connection, but Claire hadn't been able to find it.

''Make sure you bring it home tomorrow, okay?''

''It'll be too late by then.''

And whose fault would that be? Claire bit back the sarcastic comment. Criticism wouldn't help. At least, so far it hadn't.

Now Andie frowned. ''Daddy didn't say anything about going away last night when he tucked me in.''

''I think it was a last-minute trip.'' Which was sort of true, wasn't it? Claire bent down to give Andie a good-night kiss.

''I love you, Andrea.'' She ran her fingers over her daughter's soft cheek.

''Love you, too, Mom.''

BY THE TIME ALL THREE GIRLS were tucked in it was nine-thirty. Claire sat in the family room, staring at a tablet she was holding in her hand. She'd found the bottle of herbal sleeping pills sitting in the medicine cabinet. Kirk must have bought them; she'd never seen them before. Constant activity had made it possible to get through the day. But how was she going to survive the night?

She took out the sheaf of instructions and wasn't surprised when she saw that the product wasn't recommended for pregnant women. She dropped the tablet back in the bottle and wondered what to do now.

If only she could have a stiff brandy. She remembered the homemade variety a friend's mother used to make and smiled nostalgically.

Drew, Mallory and Grady. Old friends from happier days, when she and her parents had spent their summers at their luxurious cottage on Lake Rosseau, a few miles from the resort town of Port Carling. Those had been days of dreams and plans, days when the future was full of wonderful possibilities.

What would her friends say when they heard what had happened? Claire covered her face with her hands. Oh, but it was awful, and she was pregnant on top of everything.

This poor unborn child.

Claire moved her hands to her stomach. She was exhausted, but it seemed unlikely she'd be able to sleep. What she really wanted was to gather all three girls into her king-size bed—the bed she and Kirk had shared for so many years—and hold them close. All day she'd craved a few minutes alone; now that she had them, she missed her children.

The phone rang, a startling sound in the quiet house.

"Hello?"

It was Kirk. His familiar voice made her throat tighten. How many times in the past six months had he called at about this hour to tell her not to wait up for him? She held her breath, waiting to see what he wanted.

"Are the girls asleep?"

"I think so."

"Can I come over to talk?"

"No." She didn't want to see him; couldn't stand to see him.

Or was that true? Didn't a part of her long for

him to wrap her in his arms and tell her he didn't love Janice; he loved her?

"I need clothes for tomorrow, Claire. I've booked into a hotel close to the office, but I don't have anything with me. I'll have to pack a suitcase."

Claire's chest compressed with pain. A hotel. A suitcase. Just hearing him say the words made their separation all so real. This truly was happening, and it was happening to *her*.

"Whatever, Kirk. You have a key." She hung up the phone and went upstairs to make sure the girls were asleep. Looking at their soft smooth faces, relaxed in sleep, Claire felt the dampness of a single tear in the corner of her eye. She blotted it with her fingertip. Kirk would be coming soon; she wouldn't cry now.

After stopping in the girls' bathroom to let out the tepid water, she went to her bedroom. The light in the walk-in closet was on. She paused at the doorway, observing that Kirk's clothing had been pushed to one side, revealing the suitcase on wheels that he took on his business trips.

Had he moved his clothes over this morning? She didn't remember noticing when she'd vacuumed earlier.

Claire shut the door and went back downstairs. In the kitchen she warmed a mug of milk. The whir of the automatic garage opener drowned out the beeps from the microwave. She sat at the counter and watched a skin begin to form over the milk, then listened as the connecting door to the garage opened and footsteps clicked on the hardwood floor.

He paused when he saw her.

"How are you doing?"

She didn't look up. "Just peachy."

"I'm sorry, Claire."

Sorry. That was something, she supposed. She firmed her jaw and met his gaze. "What are you going to do, Kirk? Are you going to move in with her? Marry her? Have children with her?"

He closed his eyes briefly. "I don't know. I certainly haven't made any plans. How can I when you and I—"

"Do you want a divorce?" Oh, how calm she sounded. It was a miracle, when what she really wanted was to yell and scream.

"I don't know." He sounded miserable.

"I've told the girls you're away on a business trip. That'll give us a few days to decide what to say to them. And how."

She felt the second tear but didn't reach for it. Kirk wouldn't see it; the light was dim. Instead, she poked at the skin on her milk. It wrinkled and she pushed it to the edge of the mug.

She could feel Kirk's eyes on her. Watching. At that moment she realized that her romantic memories of their wedding day had been a sham. A part of her had always expected this would happen to them.

"Pack your bag, Kirk. Pack your bag and leave."

CHAPTER FOUR

ON THE LAST DAY OF SCHOOL, the girls brought home their report cards. Claire wasn't surprised when only Daisy and Jenna dug theirs eagerly out of their backpacks. She oohed and aahed over their good marks and the positive comments from their teachers. Then she turned to Andie.

"How about your report card, hon?"

"It's in here." Andie tossed a manila envelope onto the counter. "Can I have a snack? I'm starved."

"Sure. I cut up some cheese and apples." Claire opened the flap and slid out the form. The results had her catching her breath. There were three reporting dates in the school year, and Andie's grades showed a steady decline. These last results were the worst yet.

"Oh, Andie."

"I don't care." Andie bit into a piece of apple. "I don't even like school."

"But you used to *love* it."

Claire read through the teacher's comments. "Part of the reason your marks are so low is that you haven't been finishing your assignments. Andie, what has gotten into you?"

"Having to go to school all day is bad enough. Why should I have to work when I get home, too?" Andie swiveled on her stool. "When's Daddy coming home? He's been gone a long time."

Claire reached for another Granny Smith apple and carefully cut it into fours. Her daughter had neatly turned the tables with that last comment. Almost a week had passed since she'd asked Kirk to move out. After that first night he'd phoned every evening to talk to the girls. But the family couldn't go on this way indefinitely. Thank God summer holidays were here. She'd take the girls to the cottage at Lake Rosseau, as usual.

When would the girls see their father? Claire didn't want to think about that. She supposed they'd have to make some sort of arrangement.

But just the idea made her feel nauseous again.

"He'll be home soon, Andie." The words sounded reassuring, but inside, Claire knew she was a liar. Sure their father would be home soon. But for how long?

"Daddy!"

All three girls rushed for their father, who was holding a table for them at the local pizza parlor. Kirk had phoned shortly after the girls got home from school, to suggest they celebrate the end of the school year with dinner out.

"Why was your business trip so long, Daddy?" Jenna reached up to touch his face, his hair. On his other side, Andie held tightly to his free hand, while Daisy hugged him around the waist.

Claire compressed her lips and blinked, afraid that she was going to cry. Her husband, although as well dressed and handsome as usual, looked drawn. The smile he was wearing was surely forced. Over the children's heads, he sought her gaze, his gray eyes anxious and questioning.

Claire turned away, concentrating, instead, on her chair as she pulled it out and sat down. She adjusted the cutlery in front of her as Kirk kissed the girls, then pulled Jenna onto his lap.

"I've missed you, peanut." He pressed his face into her hair. "I've missed you all."

Claire knew better than to include herself in that list. She reviewed the familiar menu briefly, certain she wouldn't eat a bite. Watching the girls fall over their father was so painful. He truly was their hero, a man who could do no wrong. Claire didn't want them to lose that trust, any more than she wanted to jeopardize anything in their secure little world.

"Shirley Temples, girls?" Kirk asked when the waiter hovered.

Claire ordered a soda water.

"No beer?" Kirk asked with raised eyebrows. They always had beer with pizza.

"Not this time." She had to tell him about the baby; she knew that. At three months with Andie, her waist had still been slender. But this was her fourth child, and she was already out of any clothing with a fixed waistband. Leggings and an oversized shirt could hide a lot. But not for much longer.

Besides, the baby was a reality that had to be faced.

"So, girls," Kirk said. "How were the report cards?"

Claire noticed Andie shrink back into her seat, letting her sisters take the limelight.

"I improved in language arts and in math," Daisy said proudly.

"And my teacher said I'm a good 'tributor to group discussions," Jenna added.

Kirk laughed. "I'll just bet you are. That sounds terrific, girls. And what about Andie?"

Red curls shook from side to side. Andie's face was so low it appeared she was searching for something under the table.

"Didn't you have a good report?" Kirk glanced worriedly at Claire, then back to their eldest daughter.

"I have to go to the bathroom." Andie's voice

quavered as she slid out of her chair and ran to the back of the restaurant.

Kirk looked at Claire.

"Andie dropped grades in almost every subject except language arts." Claire pushed back her chair and threw her paper napkin on the table.

"I don't understand." Kirk frowned. Like her, he was used to academic excellence from Andie.

"It started with the March report card," Claire reminded him. "Unfortunately, her marks are even lower now. Especially in math and science. I'm going to see if I can help."

The bathroom had facilities for one person at a time, and the door was locked when Claire got there.

"Andrea?" she called gently. "Are you okay, hon?"

There was no response.

"Please let me in. We need to talk." No, not talk. What Claire really wanted was to hold her daughter in her arms. The poor child was probably upset about having disappointed her father.

The special bond between Kirk and Andie had formed in the weeks after Andie's birth. Claire's recovery from an unplanned C-section had been slow and Kirk had taken two weeks off from work to care for their new baby and his bedridden wife.

"Go away, Mom."

Knowing that Andie was hurting didn't make the

words any less wounding. Not that long ago a kiss and hug from Mommy could banish almost any problem. These days there seemed so little she could do to help.

Swallowing hard, Claire tried again. "Please, Andie. Let me in."

"Leave me alone."

Reluctantly, Claire returned to the table. The server had brought their drinks, and Jenna and Daisy were busy removing orange wedges and maraschino cherries from the little plastic swords that rested on the top of their glasses.

She glanced at Kirk, who was holding his beer but hadn't drunk any of it. "She doesn't want to talk to me."

"Let's give her a few moments," he suggested. "Let her come back on her own terms."

Claire wasn't convinced that was the right approach, but sure enough, after about ten minutes Andie reappeared and slid into her chair. The pizza had arrived by then, and Claire inched a slice of pepperoni-and-cheese onto Andie's plate.

Report cards weren't mentioned again, and the girls ate ravenously. In all the commotion, Claire doubted if anyone noticed that she did little more than tear her pizza into bits, but as they rose to leave, she found Kirk at her elbow, pulling back her chair.

"Not hungry, Claire?"

He sounded worried. For a second she closed her eyes, smelling the faint tang of his aftershave, feeling the brush of his arms against her back.

Tell me this has all been a horrible dream. Tell me this is just a normal family night out.

Tell me lies.

"Andie seems to be feeling better," he said.

She nodded. "Maybe the two of you should have a talk."

"I agree. How about tonight?"

She paused. The girls had rushed ahead to Kirk's sedan, which he'd unlocked with the remote control on his key.

"I have to come home, Claire. The girls know I'm back from that so-called business trip."

"I don't know, Kirk." It had been almost a week, yet she still felt so uncertain about which way to proceed. They had to tell the girls, but how?

"I phoned a family counselor," Kirk told her. "She said she's seen situations like ours before and she cautioned against hasty decisions. Her advice was that until we resolve the issues between us, we should try to keep things as normal as possible for the sake of the children."

"Before we decide for sure that we're getting a divorce?"

Kirk's eyes dropped. "Maybe. I don't know, Claire…"

"In other words, you want to stay married but continue to see your girlfriend."

He flushed. "All I'm asking is that we protect the kids while we're working this out."

"And that means…?"

"I move back into the house."

Claire shook her head. Having Kirk back home would be wonderful for the girls, but it would create an impossible situation for her. "Do you expect to sleep in our room? With me?"

"Wouldn't the kids think it was strange if I didn't?"

This wasn't fair. Yet she couldn't refuse. Andie, for sure, would question a move to the couch in the downstairs office.

"I suppose. For one night."

Two creases etched Kirk's forehead. "One night?"

"Tomorrow I'm taking them to the cottage for the summer."

"What about swimming lessons?"

Usually, they stayed in the city until the girls had finished two weeks of swimming lessons at the local community center. "I think we'll skip them this year."

Kirk's eyes were a smoky gray. In a good mood, they lightened to the silvery hue of weathered cedar. In more serious moods, like now, they reminded her of the summer storm clouds over the cottage on hot, humid evenings.

"I'm going to want to see them every weekend," he said.

"That'll be more than other summers."

CLAIRE FOLDED AND SORTED the girls' laundry in the master bedroom while Kirk got them settled for the night. The door was open and she could hear the familiar sounds from down the hall as the girls put on jammies and brushed their teeth, all much more willingly for Kirk than when she was supervising.

"I have a loose tooth, Daddy," Daisy said.

"So do I," added Jenna. "My first one! Is it ready to come out?"

"Let's see." There was a pause as Kirk no doubt examined the tooth in question. "Not quite yet. Maybe a few more weeks, Jenna. Yours looks close, though, Daisy. Should we try the string trick?"

"No, no..." Daisy didn't like blood.

"Okay," Kirk said. "We don't have to do that. It'll come out on its own. Boy, the tooth fairy sure is going to be busy around this house, isn't she?"

"Da-ad." This came, condescendingly, from Andie.

"What?" Kirk asked, his voice all innocence.

A door slammed. Claire added Daisy's soft yellow sweatshirt to a pile and smiled. She could just imagine the expression that had preceded Andie's dramatic departure.

"Okay." Kirk clapped his hands. "I'll tuck Daisy in first, then I'll sing Jenna her songs. After that we're going to have a little talk, Andie."

There were muffled words from behind the closed door.

Claire took Andie's pile of clothes, passing Kirk in the hallway as he followed Daisy to her room.

"Excuse me." She lowered her head and angled her body to edge by him. For a moment she thought his gaze settled on her thickening middle, but he didn't say anything. She tapped on Andie's door.

"Here's your laundry. I even found a pair of jeans in the basket today—I can't imagine how that happened."

The room was dark already, and Andie was settled in bed. Clearly, she wasn't in the mood to be teased. Was she ever these days?

Claire put the clothes in the dresser, then paused at the head of the bed and stroked Andie's forehead. "Are you okay, honey?"

Andie blinked. "Is Daddy going to be mad at me?"

"Why would he be?"

"Because of my grades."

Claire sighed and sat down. Andie was as sensitive to the opinions of others, especially her father, as her fair skin was to the sun. "Do you think you tried your hardest at school this year?"

Andie pulled the covers over her face, leaving just her pale blue eyes exposed. "I don't know."

"Maybe you're a little disappointed yourself with your grades?"

Andie's face reddened; her eyes filled with tears.

Claire bent over to kiss her cheek. "I love you, Andrea."

"I love you, too, Mom."

"We're going to have a great summer. Have you decided which friend you'd like to invite to join us for a few weeks? You and Courtney had a lot of fun last year."

Andie was silent for a while, then she turned to face the opposite wall. "I don't want to invite anyone."

Lately, it was always like this whenever Claire tried to suggest an outing or a sleepover with a friend. "But, Andie—"

"I just want it to be family. Okay? I see enough of my friends at school and soccer."

"Are you sure? I've noticed you don't enjoy playing with your sisters as much as you used to."

"Just family," she insisted. "Is Daddy coming with us to the cottage?"

"You know he has to work. But he'll be there weekends."

With a final parting kiss, Claire left to get Daisy's clothes. Daisy was burrowed under her quilt when Claire walked in the room.

"Guess what I am, Mom?"

"A bear hibernating in winter?" Claire opened a drawer and put away Daisy's underwear.

Giggles erupted from under the covers. "Nope."

"An archeologist exploring a cave?"

"Wrong again!"

"I give up."

"I'm a tooth!" She lifted the covers high over her head. "See? The covers are my mouth."

Claire laughed and brushed her hand over Daisy's mop. "No chewing the sheets, okay? Even teeth need to rest now and then. Good night, Daisy."

Back in the hall, Claire was stopped cold by the sound of Kirk singing a traditional Irish lullaby to Jenna.

Too-ra-loo-ra-loo-ra, Hush now don't you cry.

Tears stung, and her breath caught in her throat. His voice was so gentle, so full of promises he must know he couldn't keep. On the last line he lost it, paused, then started again on a wobbly, false note. Jenna covered for him, her baby voice on key. And then it was over.

"That's okay, Daddy," Jenna quickly reassured him. "It's a sad song, isn't it, Daddy?"

LATER, CLAIRE UNDRESSED in the bathroom off the master bedroom. When she emerged, she had her old terry robe hanging loosely around her, belt undone so she wouldn't draw attention to her middle.

Kirk was already in bed, reading by the light of a bedside lamp. He looked up when he saw her, and she was suddenly dry mouthed, aware of him in a way she hadn't been in years. Kirk's job was sedentary, but he kept in shape by swimming three mornings a week, and as a result his upper body was still powerful, with well-defined muscles and no excess body weight.

Her own exercise routine consisted of jogging up and down the stairs about a hundred times a day, yet somehow she didn't seem to achieve the same results.

Careful to avoid eye contact, Claire went to her side of the bed. Kirk always slept in a pair of boxer shorts, but given the change in their circumstances, she'd thought he'd add a T-shirt, as well. Apparently, he'd seen no need for anything different.

She had. Instead of her usual silky teddy, she'd chosen the long cotton nightgown the girls had given her last Mother's Day.

After unfastening her watch, she slid her housecoat over her shoulders. Still facing the wall, she said, "This is too weird."

"Just sleep with your back toward me. It isn't as if you haven't had the practice."

"What?" She glanced back at him. "Are you trying to say this is my fault?"

"No." He sighed. "No."

It was all so unfair. Their life was in ruins, and Kirk lay there reading in bed as though nothing had happened. "What about Janice? How does she feel about you sleeping at the house with me?"

"Janice knows I'm married."

Anger flashed inside her. Of course Janice knew he was married. Hadn't Claire served the woman beef tenderloin with five-pepper sauce in this very house? To think she had actually fussed over the timing of a chocolate soufflé for that woman. And served it with an absolutely flawless vanilla sauce. If she'd only known. Gelatin would have been too good....

But why blame Janice? Kirk was the one she was married to; Kirk was the one who'd vowed his fidelity.

Claire turned off the light on her side of the bed. The truth was, Kirk was a successful, good-looking guy. His meticulous attention to detail could drive a person crazy at times, but he was also an incredibly patient man, capable of great tenderness.

No wonder Janice had thrown caution aside and fallen in love with him. Her marriage was over; she had nothing to lose.

"Claire?"

She half turned, and watched as Kirk removed the glasses he used for reading.

"I'm as confused as you are right now. If we could only talk…"

So he could tell her more details about his affair with Janice? Or explain how the affair was really *Claire's* fault? She shook her head.

"What about with a counselor present? Would that make you feel more comfortable?"

Claire wrapped her arms around her middle. She didn't need a counselor to understand that she couldn't stay married to a man who was in love with another woman.

And she wasn't too impressed with the advice Kirk had received so far. Sure they had to protect the children, but this sleeping in the same bed was ridiculous.

"I just don't see the use in talking. What's it going to change?" She pulled the housecoat back over her shoulders and stood.

"Where are you going?"

"To the couch, downstairs."

"But the girls…"

"I'll be up before they're awake." If she even went to sleep, that is.

"Then let me be the one to sleep downstairs." Kirk whipped off the covers, and she saw that he *was* wearing his boxers.

"I prefer it this way," she insisted, heading for

the door. "The truth is, I haven't been able to sleep in this room all week."

"Really?" His voice broke on the word. "Oh, Claire. I'm so sorry."

Good, she thought, he ought to be sorry. But that didn't stop the tears from rushing to her eyes. She'd been so strong that first day; she must have been in shock. Lately, she could do little more than cry. Often, she had to turn her back to the children, walk into a different room so they wouldn't notice.

"I never..." Kirk didn't finish his thought, but his expression was tormented. Claire didn't want to feel sorry for him; she *couldn't* feel sorry for him. He'd made his choices, and now they all had to face the consequences.

"How could you?" The words burst out, even though she'd told herself there was no point in asking. Kirk flinched.

"I don't know."

Anger struck like white lightning, jolting her body rigid. "That's just not good enough, Kirk."

And she left, closing the door behind her.

CHAPTER FIVE

BEHIND THE WHEEL of her forest-green minivan, Claire felt better than she had all week. It was summer, the sky was blue and she was headed to her favorite place in the entire world.

Muskoka lake country. Just a few hours north of Toronto, fertile plains gave way to the rock and trees and lakes of the Canadian Shield. There were well over a thousand lakes in the twenty-five-hundred square miles of cottage country that stretched from Georgian Bay to Algonquin Park, but the big ones were Muskoka, Rosseau and Joseph, and the little resort town of Port Carling sat at the apex of all three.

Port Carling was home to several of Claire's closest friends. Mallory Driscoll, who ran a trendy boutique on Steamboat Bay; her husband, Drew, who owned, published and edited the *Hub of the Lakes Gazette*; and their two-year-old daughter, Angel, named for Drew's mother, Angela, who'd passed away several years ago.

Then there was Grady Hogan. Newly divorced, the father of twin adolescent boys, Grady was

Claire's teenage sweetheart, the first love of her life.

Muskoka. To Claire the name conjured happy memories of her oldest and dearest friends. A place of simple pleasures and long, lazy days that seemed to last forever. A place of startling contrasts like the shock of her body slicing through cold, bracing water, after hours spent baking in the hot, humid air. Or the daylight sounds of laughter traveling over water and the thrumming of motorboat engines, compared with the early-morning song of the loons and the plaintive call of an owl at midnight.

From the time she was a baby, her family had spent their summers at their cottage on Lake Rosseau. Claire had grown up on the smell of woodlands and lake water. Her favorite foods were summertime foods—corn fresh off the husk, blueberries sprinkled with sugar, spicy smokies barbecued on an open bonfire.

When her parents retired and moved to Florida, they'd deeded the place to Claire, and the tradition of summer at the cottage continued with the next generation. Usually, her mom and dad came up for a couple of weeks in the summer, but this year they'd opted to visit Claire's aunt on Vancouver Island, instead.

Just as well. Claire didn't want them to know

about the problems between her and Kirk until they'd been settled. One way or another.

"I'm going to learn to water-ski this year," Daisy announced.

Last year Andie had mastered the technique, much to her younger sisters' chagrin.

"Well, I'm going to learn to drop a ski," Andie said.

"Provided Grady has time to take us out on his boat," Claire cautioned. Their own motorboat didn't have the horsepower for skiing.

"Well, why wouldn't he?" Andie asked. "He's taken us every other year."

"Yes, I know. He *probably* will. I just don't think we should assume anything before we've asked."

Grady's divorce from his high-school sweetheart, Bess, had just become finalized a few months ago, and over the phone he'd sounded so depressed. And worried about the twins. Initially, Warren and Taylor had felt as if their mother had abandoned them, too, when she left to start a new life for herself in Barrie.

Claire didn't blame them. She'd never liked Bess much; now she liked her even less. How could she leave behind her own boys? She'd said they didn't need her anymore, but Warren and Taylor had only been fifteen at the time. And what about Grady? Claire couldn't imagine any woman in her right mind leaving a husband like Grady. He was a real honey, a great guy. He hadn't deserved to be treated so badly.

And neither do I.

It was hard to believe she was now in the same category as her stalwart friend. Only, she hadn't lost her husband because he wanted to find himself. She'd lost him because of another woman.

Claire blinked behind her sunglasses, thinking of Kirk standing in the driveway, waving goodbye to them. He'd looked sad at the time, but what had he done once they were gone? Phoned Janice? Was he with her right now?

She couldn't stand to think about it.

"Can we stop for a burger?" Andie asked.

Claire glanced in the rearview mirror, seeking out her daughter's eyes. "We just had breakfast."

"But we always stop at Weber's...."

"Yeah, Mom," added Daisy.

"Well, maybe we could get milkshakes."

"And fries?" Jenna pressed.

It *was* a good idea, Claire convinced herself, pulling off the highway fifteen minutes later. She needed to eat for her unborn child, and a milkshake would go down easily. She still had so little appetite. And this morning, with Kirk at the breakfast table—well, she hadn't been able to swallow a bite.

She'd noticed him watching her, and caught his

surprise when she'd refused even coffee. He'd had three cups.

"I've been living on the stuff," he'd admitted when the girls were brushing their teeth.

She'd been perversely glad to see that his eyes looked as tired as hers, despite the extra jolts of caffeine.

How much time was he spending with Janice? Claire wouldn't allow herself to ask the question, though she burned with resentment. Sure, Kirk was upset; maybe he was even having trouble sleeping and eating, as she was. But there was someone else in his life, whereas she was alone. Did the two of them talk about her? she wondered.

Claire opened her purse on the counter as she placed her order. "Two chocolate, one strawberry and one vanilla shake." She felt Jenna tug on her arm. "Plus an order of fries."

"Three blondies and one redhead." The woman behind the till peered at Andie. "Where did you come from?"

Andie flushed a deep red. She turned her back to the counter and muttered, "The planet Carrot-top."

Claire put one hand on her daughter's shoulder and took her change with the other. "Sensitive topic," she said, knowing the woman hadn't meant to be unkind.

The four of them sat outside at one of the numerous picnic tables. Claire passed out the shakes and put the fries in the center of the table for everyone to share. Three hands reached out simultaneously. A second later Daisy's forehead creased and she placed a hand over her mouth.

"Oh, no," she mumbled from behind her hand.

"What is it?"

Daisy's eyes opened wide. Reaching inside her mouth, she plucked out something that looked like a misshapen pearl.

"My tooth came out."

"Is it bleeding?" Jenna leaned in close for a better view. "Can I see the hole? Did it hurt?"

Watching Daisy field her sisters' questions and display her trophy carefully, Claire thought how rare it was for her middle daughter to be the center of attention. Quieter than Jenna, less truculent than Andie—especially lately—she rarely caused trouble.

Claire reached across the table to stroke Daisy's cheek. "Another tooth gone. My baby is growing up."

Jenna was affronted. "*I'm* your baby, Mom."

"All three of you are my babies."

"Andie's not a baby."

"To me she is. That's just the way mothers feel about their children, Jenna." Claire looked back at Daisy, who was gliding her tongue in and out of the empty space in her mouth.

"I wonder what that gem will fetch on the tooth-fairy market?"

Daisy suddenly seemed worried. "Could I wait until next weekend to put my tooth under the pillow? I don't want the tooth fairy to take it away until Daddy gets to see it."

The sweet moment she'd been sharing with her daughters suddenly turned sour. Daddy. Did Kirk have any idea how important he was to these girls?

The fries were gone, and Claire pushed aside her unfinished milkshake. "It's time we hit the road. You can finish your drinks in the van."

"How much farther?" Jenna asked as she climbed into the middle-row seat, next to the window. They'd bought the van when she was born, and the built-in car seats had been a lifesaver. Now Claire made sure all three girls were buckled in properly before she jumped into the driver's seat.

"You know, Andie..." she began, once they were back on the highway. In the rearview mirror she saw her daughter spit out a strand of her hair, and had to choke back a reprimand. "Daddy and I were talking this morning and we decided it would be a good idea if you spent half an hour every day on that math workbook your teacher recommended."

"What? But it's summer holidays, Mom. Why do I have to do math?"

"I think you know why."

"That's not fair. I've been waiting for summer for ages. When's Daddy coming to the cottage?"

"Oh, probably next weekend," Claire said vaguely.

Thinking about Kirk driving up for the weekend made the milkshake in Claire's stomach curdle. She'd avoided the issue when Kirk had brought up the subject, yet she didn't see how she could deny him the right to visit the girls. Of course she didn't want to do that. *She* just didn't want to see him.

She scanned the horizon, noting the change in the scenery. Picturesque dairy farms and cornfields had given way to the hardy mixed forest of spruce, pine, maple and oak. They were well past Barrie, almost to Gravenhurst, but traffic was still steady on the four-lane highway. Obviously, they weren't the only family escaping pavement and pollution for the summer months.

Claire tucked her hair behind her ear and sighed. She'd driven this route so many times, yet never with such mixed feelings. She was so eager to get to their destination, to see the familiar roofline of the cottage peeking out from the surrounding trees at the bottom of the short, winding lane.

To her, the cottage felt more like home than any of the neighborhoods she'd lived in in Toronto, including the brick bungalow in Leaside where she'd been raised, the basement apartment she'd shared with a girlfriend in College Park during university and the two-story house she and Kirk had bought nine years ago in the suburb of Richmond Hill.

Of course, *cottage* was hardly the word for the spacious, well-finished bungalow that hugged the rock face along the lake's edge.

The living and dining areas opened to a fully equipped modern kitchen. A short hallway off the kitchen led to three large bedrooms and a bath and a half. The view of the lake was spectacular and sliding doors permitted access to an expansive, multitiered deck designed to connect the cottage to the water. A large dock and boathouse were the center points of most sunny afternoons.

Claire could imagine sitting there right now, her feet dangling in the cool water, the hot sun on her shoulder blades, a cold beer—no, make that a lemonade—in her hand.

She thought of her husband, as she did a hundred times every day, wondering what he was experiencing. Was he relieved that the truth was finally out in the open? Was he feeling guilt, sorrow, pain?

She knew that he must be, but somehow she always imagined him with Janice, laughing and at ease.

It was so damn unfair.

Part of her was happy to put as many miles between Kirk and herself as she could. But that didn't stop her from missing him and wondering if she was wise to leave him alone and free to focus all his time on Janice.

What was the right thing to do?

She wished she knew.

CLAIRE WAS OPENING WINDOWS to freshen up the bedrooms, when she heard a vehicle in the drive. A moment later, a voice called from the screen door.

"Claire? Are you in there?"

It was Mallory. Her heart lightening, Claire grabbed a tissue and rushed out to greet her, pausing when she saw Mallory's reaction to her appearance.

"Claire." Mallory sounded shocked. "You've been crying."

She couldn't deny it. She was just thankful the girls had been outside playing when she'd stepped into her and Kirk's bedroom and seen the book of poetry he'd bought her just last summer. She'd picked up the slim volume and opened it to his inscription: *You are lovelier than any poem.*

The words had stung with their beauty, and tears had followed quickly. There in her hands was the evidence that he had loved her once. What had happened to change that?

"Are you okay?" Mallory held out her arms, and Claire stepped into them for a hug.

"No." She squeezed tightly, then sat back on the edge of the sofa, pulling Mallory with her. "I'm sorry. Usually, I manage to keep myself together, but today for some reason..."

"What do you mean, keep yourself together? Oh, I knew something was wrong when you phoned to say you'd be here earlier than usual. You didn't sound like yourself." Mallory put her arm over Claire's shoulders.

"It's Kirk."

"Is he working too much again?"

"Not this time."

"Then what?"

Mallory sounded anxious, and Claire's stomach churned like lake water caught up in a boat propeller. So far she hadn't told a soul about her and Kirk's problems. Now it was a relief to finally confide, "He's fallen in love with another woman."

"No." Mallory's body went rigid. "Are you sure?"

Claire felt the tears begin to gather again. "He told me himself."

"The bastard." Mallory wrapped both arms around Claire. "How could he do that? Why would he do something like that?"

Quickly, Claire went through the whole story. The other woman's divorce, the innocent lunches that had led to not-so-innocent dinners, open meetings turning suddenly secret. "He says they haven't slept together."

"Well, that's something."

"If it's true. He *loves* her, Mallory. Do you know how long it's been since he told me he loved me? Months."

Claire swung her bare feet, and noticed the chipped pink polish.

"Oh, Claire. I can't stand that this is happening to you. Have you said anything to the girls?"

"No. I just don't know how I'll ever find the strength. Mallory, they'll be devastated. Kirk isn't around as much as they'd like, but they adore him."

"Of course they do." Mallory patted her arm.

"Kirk says we need to talk, but I don't know what that will accomplish. I've asked him if he wants a d-divorce, but he seems almost as confused as I am."

"Oh, Claire…"

"How's Grady doing?" Claire asked, the topic of divorce making her think of their mutual friend.

"Oh, he's finally out of that terrible depression. He's even started dating again. I think up until the day the divorce was official, he kept hoping Bess would change her mind."

"I bet the twins were hoping the same thing." Claire kept staring at her feet. "Who's he dating?"

"Remember the woman Drew and I found living in the MacDougals' cottage two winters ago?"

Claire remembered. Drew had written an outstanding editorial on the subject of homelessness. The woman had just left an abusive relationship and had no money or source of income, so she and her young daughter had been reduced to taking shelter in various cottages that had been closed for the winter.

What was her name? "Terese Balfour?"

"Yes. She's the guidance counselor at Warren and Taylor's school now, and believe me, Grady and she have been doing a lot of talking in the past few years."

"Are the twins okay?"

"They're a lot better. They're still covering high-school sports for Drew at the *Gazette*. And I think they've finally started seeing their mom on a regular basis again."

"How old are they? Seventeen? I can hardly believe it."

"I know. They both have driver's licenses. Next year they'll be off to college."

"Incredible." Claire put her hands on her bare knees. A cool breeze was wafting through all the open windows and now she felt cold. She grabbed an old afghan and wrapped it around her. "Are Grady and Terese serious?"

"I'm not sure. Grady really likes her, but Terese's experience with her ex-husband has left her cautious, to say the least. She's pretty scared about getting involved in a serious relationship. And she's worried about her daughter. Lisa just dotes on Grady, and Terese's concerned she might get too attached.''

"Sounds complicated.''

"Nothing's as simple as it should be,'' Mallory said.

"Except for you, Drew and Angel.'' Claire smiled, forcing her thoughts from her own troubled situation. "Does Drew ever regret quitting the rat race in Ottawa to run the *Gazette*?''

"He claims he couldn't be happier. And I know I couldn't.'' Mallory smoothed a hand over the afghan, then raised anxious eyes to her friend.

"Drew says I see the world through rose-colored glasses, but I can't help feeling shaken. Only two years ago I looked at you and Kirk and Grady and Bess and thought you all had the world in your hands. Now Grady and Bess are divorced. And you and Kirk—'' Mallory covered her face with her hands. "I'm sorry.''

"Don't be.'' Claire put her arm around Mallory and hugged her close. "It *is* horrible. No one knows it more than me.''

Mallory's breath shuddered. "Oh, Claire. Does happily ever after even exist anymore?''

CHAPTER SIX

KIRK ALWAYS CALLED whenever Claire took the girls up to the cottage by herself, to make sure they'd arrived safely. Would he this time? Maybe he was enjoying his new freedom too much to spare them a second thought.

Claire struck a match and held it to the ball of scrunched-up newspaper she'd placed under a stack of kindling. Immediately, a small orange flame sprang to life against the edge of the paper and began traveling upward. Soon, the paper was engulfed in flames, and the small chips of cedar began to spark.

"Are we ready for the logs?" Daisy asked. All the girls, even little two-year-old Angel, had carried armfuls of dried, split wood from the shed to the fire pit next to the boat dock.

"We can start with a few of the smaller ones. Do you want to put them on? Be careful." Claire stood back as each girl added one of the thinner chunks of wood. Andie held Angel's hand as the little girl threw a small square of cedar at the fire.

Andie was good with Angel. Claire sought out

Mallory, who was watching the scene from the comfort of one of the four wooden outdoor chairs that sat in a semicircle around the pit. She was eyeing her daughter with a serene smile; it was obvious she trusted Andie to keep her safe.

How would Andie feel about a new sister or brother? And what about Daisy and Jenna? So much change coming all at once. Claire didn't know how they were going to cope. She still hadn't told a soul about the baby, and thought longingly of confiding in Mallory. The girls had interrupted their earlier conversation before she'd had a chance to bring up this added complication in her life.

Maybe later they could speak privately again, after the sun had begun to set, when the kids had had their fill of hot dogs and the fire had burned down to a mass of orange-blue coals.

The wiener roast was a tradition for the first night of summer vacation, dating back when Claire had been a little girl. Now the familiar smell of burning wood brought back the secure feeling of sitting between her parents, her face warmed by the fire, two whole months of swimming, boating and playing with her friends ahead of her.

She hoped her children would remember these times with the same fondness. Later, after the hot dogs, they'd make s'mores, sandwiching roasted marshmallows and squares of chocolate between graham-wafer cookies. And then would come hot chocolate and bedtime stories, and not a word about baths, although she would make the girls brush their teeth.

"Can we start cooking the hot dogs?" Jenna asked. Her little chin was smeared with dirt, and her pink T-shirt was covered with chips of bark and wood splinters.

"No, hon. We have to build a great big fire, then wait until it turns to coals. Why don't you play for a while. Then it won't seem like so long to wait."

Claire went back into the cottage to get the tray of food she and Mallory had assembled earlier. Mallory followed, bringing the huge container of lemonade and the stackable plastic glasses.

"Did you invite Grady and the boys?" she asked.

"I did. How about Drew? Is he coming?"

"Any minute," Mallory assured her. "He's been working really hard on this issue of the *Gazette,* since it marks the beginning of the summer season. I know he's going to want to talk to you about it when he gets here."

"Why me?"

"I'll let him explain."

"You tease." Claire set the tray down on the large round cedar table, then added several of the larger logs to the fire. It was burning briskly now, snapping and crackling in the calm, pretwilight air.

The breeze from earlier in the day had died

down, and the low sun cast long shadows over the smooth, calm lake. Claire filled her lungs with lake-country air and told herself nothing could ever be too bad, as long as she had this place and her children. She could hear them now, laughing and shouting as they played hide-and-seek in the tall trees and low-lying brush.

"I'm counting to ten! One, two, three…"

Claire lit several citronella candles to discourage the mosquitoes, then began to organize the food. She had plain wieners for the children, spicy smokies for the adults. A tray of cut-up veggies and dip sat in the center of the table, and the makings for the s'mores lay covered with a tea towel.

"Relax, Claire," Mallory said. "Why don't you sit for a minute."

"I can't," Claire admitted. If she wasn't busy she would start thinking about Kirk and wondering why he hadn't called. She'd placed her cell phone on the table so she wouldn't miss the call if he phoned. Wasn't that pathetic?

Tires crunching on dirt and gravel caught both her and Mallory's attention. Out of the woods came the four girls, all running in anticipation.

"Uncle Drew!" Claire's girls yelled, spying the familiar Explorer that had once belonged to Drew's mother, Angie. Angie's death, almost three years ago now, had prompted Drew's return to Port Carling, but it was Mallory and their baby, Angel, who'd convinced him to stay. He'd left a promising career as a journalist, although he still hosted a program on foreign affairs for the national public radio station, which was broadcast Thursday evenings from Toronto.

"Warren and Taylor!" Daisy shrieked, seeing Grady's old truck right behind. One of the twins was driving, Claire noted, sitting almost as tall as his father beside him.

Quickly, she added the last of the logs to the fire, then joined the welcoming committee as they exchanged hugs and kisses and hellos.

"Hey, Drew, looking good," she said as Mallory's husband threw an arm around her shoulder. His short dark hair was as bristly as ever, and his chin scratched when he bent to kiss her cheek.

"Good to see you, Claire. How's Kirk doing? Sorry sod, stuck in the big city...."

Claire blinked and forced a dry laugh, then turned to Grady. He wore a blue-and-gray plaid shirt and jeans, his boyish grin lighting up his face. His medium-brown hair was on the long side, and he brushed it back with an impatient gesture a second before his gaze fell on her.

"Claire." He squeezed her tight, and she fought the urge to bury her face against his strong shoulder. She could smell his workshop in his shirt. Grady built and repaired motorboats, specializing in custom wooden craft. It was good, honest work, which left him time to join his family for dinner, to spend his weekends fishing and waterskiing. If only Kirk...

She glanced at the phone, still sitting silently on the table, then went to say hello to the twins.

"Hi, Warren, Taylor. I hope the girls aren't going to drive you crazy. They've been so excited about seeing you."

Taylor gave her a shy smile. "It's okay," he said. Warren just shrugged and glanced at his father.

When they were younger, the boys had been incredibly patient and kind with the girls, but over the past few years their attitudes had shifted. It was to be expected, given their ages, and Claire had tried to warn her daughters that Grady's boys might not want to play with them.

But now they agreed to a game of hide-and-seek, with both of them being "it."

"Be back in fifteen minutes," Claire called out as six small figures disappeared into the darkening woods. "The fire should be ready by then."

"Come sit down," Drew said. "I want to talk to you."

Claire remembered what Mallory had said earlier. "Okay. But let me get you a beer first."

"Grady's ahead of you," Drew said, holding up a tin from a local brewery. "He's gone to put the rest of the six-pack in the fridge."

Claire perched on the wide arm of Drew's chair. "Okay. What is it?"

"I wondered how you'd feel about starting up the 'Cottage Cooking' column for the paper this summer."

The offer surprised Claire. She didn't know what she'd expected, but writing a column… Shifting her gaze to the horizon, she noticed the sun was about to slip behind the barely visible trees on the other side of the lake. Gold-and-orange fingers of color skimmed the gentle swells that rippled the water's surface.

"The 'Cottage Cooking' column," she repeated softly. Drew had discontinued it after his mother's death, and she'd missed its homey presence in the weekly paper.

"I can't afford to pay you much," Drew said. "But I will pay."

"I know you gave Angie half the recipes she used to print," Mallory added. It was common knowledge that Angie herself hadn't much of a cook.

"Yes, but Angie always wrote such charming stories to go with them."

"I'm sure you'll develop your own style," Drew said reassuringly. "Come on, Claire. I appreciate that the girls keep you busy, but won't you at least give it a try?"

Claire had worked in the hospitality industry be-

fore her children were born. Now she'd been out
of the workforce for over ten years. Not that one
column for a local paper constituted much in the
way of work.

Besides, the girls were older now. Even her baby
was six, and constantly reminding her that she
could "do it herself." Maybe this was a good idea.
Maybe it would help keep her busy and her mind
off other things....

"Okay. Sure. I'll give it a try."

"Starting this week?" Drew asked coaxingly.
"I'd really like to have a column for the first summer issue." He glanced at Mallory, then added
quickly, "Although next week would be okay,
too."

"I'll try for this week," Claire decided. Strawberries would be ripening soon, and she had her
own variation of the ever-popular strawberry shortcake. That ought to be a good starting point.

"Great! I knew I could count on you."

"I brought you girls a beer," Grady said, just
back from the cottage. He tossed a can to Mallory,
then another to Claire.

Claire set hers back on the table regretfully. If
ever a woman could have used a drink, it was she,
especially after this past week. "I'll stick to lemonade for tonight." As she poured herself a glass
she was aware that all three of them were watching
her. She turned and leaned up against the table.

"Okay. What is it?"

"You just said no to a beer," Grady said, exchanging a meaningful nod with Drew. "There are only three other times you ever turned down the first beer of the summer."

"Any coincidence that she also has three little girls playing in the woods right now?" Drew inquired, lowering his voice a notch.

"Don't tease," Mallory said. "So what if she doesn't feel like a beer. You guys read too much into the simplest things."

"Do we?"

The light was fading, but Claire could feel them inspecting her. She resisted the urge to smooth down her white T-shirt, to try to hide the expanding waistline that was so obvious to her.

"It's true," she said quietly. "I'm pregnant. But the girls don't know." She took a deep breath. "Even Kirk doesn't know."

She stared into the heart of the fire, where the wood seemed to be glowing from within. It was perfect for roasting wieners now. She should call the kids. And she would. In a minute.

What were her friends thinking? She knew they'd be exchanging stunned glances, although no one had yet said a word. Then she felt Grady's arm around her shoulder.

"I take it there's a reason you haven't told Kirk?"

She nodded, then turned her head into his chest, unable to say another word without crying. Drew came up on her other side, then Mallory.

"It'll be okay, Claire," she said. "I just know it will."

Claire pressed her lips together and nodded. With the back of her hand, she brushed away the moisture that had collected along her eyelashes. After a deep breath, she straightened.

"Th-thanks, guys. I hope you're right." But what were the chances? Her husband didn't love her anymore. He loved someone else. How could any marriage survive something like that?

"How about we call the kids in from their game," Mallory suggested gently. "The fire looks about right, doesn't it?"

"Perfect," Grady said, gently wiping Claire's cheek with one callused finger.

At that moment the phone rang. Claire stared at it, not sure she wanted to answer. It had to be Kirk. Who else would call on her cell phone? But she wasn't sure she could talk to him right now.

"Is the fire ready?" Andie came tearing out from behind the woodshed, still holding Angel's hand. "I'm *starving!*"

"Me, too!" Angel said.

"And me!"

"And me!"

Claire reached for the wooden sticks that Kirk

had carved several years ago, but Mallory took them out of her hand.

"We'll get the kids organized," she said. "You answer the phone." Then she placed the slim piece of black plastic into Claire's hand.

Turning her back on the fire and the noise of four hungry children and two hungry teens, Claire pressed the talk button.

"Hello?"

"Claire? I was beginning to worry. Did the trip go okay?"

Kirk's voice sounded so thin and fragile. Claire tried to picture his face, his body. Where was he? At home? The office? With Janice?

"The trip went fine. We stopped for milk-shakes." It was such a trivial detail she immediately felt silly for mentioning it. But suddenly she longed to tell him every single thing they'd done since leaving that morning.

"Sounds nice," he said. "I wish…"

She hung on, waiting for the end of that sentence, but he didn't finish.

"I'd like to come up this weekend," he said. "To see the girls."

Claire stepped farther away from the gathering, until she was certain no one could hear her. "I'm not sure that's a good idea."

"Why not?"

Oh, how could she explain? This was the one

place she felt safe, protected. Where she could pretend, just for a little while, that everything was still normal. If he drove up to the cottage, all that peace of mind would be lost to her.

"I need to see the girls, Claire. I miss them already."

What about me? Claire put a hand to her chest and closed her eyes. She would not cry. Not on the phone, not talking to him. She had to be strong. And she had to think of the girls. He was right. Their interests must be put first.

"Then I guess you'd better come. When should I tell the girls to expect you?"

"How about Saturday morning?"

Usually he came Friday night. But maybe he'd reserved that time to spend with Janice.

"Fine."

"We'll talk then, Claire. We need to make some decisions."

Claire didn't want to make decisions. She wanted a husband who loved her. A father for her three girls and for the unborn child she carried inside her.

When she didn't answer, Kirk said, "I'll see you Saturday, then. Give my love to the girls."

Claire turned off the power on the cell phone and fought for her composure. She couldn't break down now, not even with Mallory, Drew and

Grady to cover for her. She'd seen Andie look at her when the phone had started ringing.

She had to return to the fire and pretend all was normal.

Oh, why was this happening to her?

CHAPTER SEVEN

CLAIRE SPENT THE NEXT MORNING working on her strawberry-shortcake recipe with the girls. After lunch she drove them all into Port Carling, where she dropped her column off at the *Gazette* with just a pang of nervousness.

"How about we stop for an ice-cream cone at Marg's Pastry Shop," she proposed. She was hoping to lighten the mood after Andie's tantrum just an hour earlier.

The morning had started promisingly enough, with Andie completing the first two pages of her math workbook much more quickly and accurately than one would expect from a student with below-average math grades.

And she'd been cooperative in the kitchen as she'd thickened frozen strawberries for the center layer of the shortcake.

Only later, while they were sampling the results, had she thrown her fit. "Why did we make Daddy's favorite dessert, when he isn't even here to have any?" She'd run to her room and stayed there until it was time to leave for Port Carling.

Claire gave Andie money for the cones, then sat in a booth to wait. The real issue wasn't the strawberry shortcake, of course. Was it boredom? It seemed to Claire that Andie spent far too much time on her own, reading. If only there were another young girl Andie's age nearby…

"Problems?" Grady slid into the bench seat across from her.

"Hey, Grady." She smiled. "Just a little kid trouble."

"Any kid in particular?"

"Andie." Claire told him about Andie's declining marks. "The problems started shortly after she had a falling-out with a friend named Erin."

"Was it a big fight?"

"I'm not sure. According to Andie, they just got bored with each other, but I don't know…."

"That happens."

"True. But Andie has other friends, friends of hers since kindergarten. And she hasn't been interested in any of them for a long time, either."

"Sounds like there's more going on here."

"I agree. But Andie won't talk to me, and her teacher swears she's seen no evidence of any problems in the classroom or on the playground. No teasing or bullying or anything of that nature."

"Taylor went through a phrase once where he just wanted to be on his own. He never was as social as his brother."

"If Andie wants time to herself, that's just fine with me. As long as she's happy..." But Claire didn't think that Andie *was* happy. In fact, the very opposite seemed true. Not wanting to burden Grady further with her problems, she changed the subject.

"How are Taylor and Warren doing, by the way? Do they still enjoy reporting on high-school sports for the *Gazette*?"

"That job has been a lifesaver. Keeps them busy nights and weekends." Grady glanced around the small café as if looking for someone, before focusing back on her, grinning in his old familiar way.

"Just think of the trouble we got into at their age, then multiply it by two, and that about sums it up."

"I was an only child, but I guess I gave my parents their share of gray hairs."

"And I helped." Grady's grin widened, and Claire wondered if he was thinking about the summer before their last year of high school, when the two of them had dated. Two glorious, wonderful months. In the fall Claire had returned to Toronto, but they'd stayed in touch—until Grady's old girlfriend found out she was pregnant, and claimed Grady as the father.

"But you can't marry Bess," Claire had argued. "It would be a terrible mistake." After all, he'd broken up with Bess, hadn't he? And he was crazy about Claire.

Just as she was crazy about him.

She remembered how he'd set her heart to pounding just by brushing his fingers on the back of her neck or placing a hand gently on her thigh. He had such a light touch, yet he was so confident, so sure. She'd been as pliant as biscuit dough in his hands, and never had she regretted that he'd been her first.

But he'd left her for Bess, and the two of them married a week after graduation. Claire couldn't even remember the name of the guy she'd ended up taking to grad. Since it couldn't be Grady, it hadn't really mattered.

She'd gone to college, then gotten a job at the Sheraton Centre in downtown Toronto. That was where she'd met Kirk. His firm held its annual Christmas dinner and dance in the Dominion Ballroom, and she'd been the special-events coordinator at the time.

And look what that had led to—

"Mom, can we eat our cones outside?" Daisy asked, skipping back from the counter with a very generous kiddie-size cone.

"Sure. Was there any change?"

Andie dropped a few coins to the table.

"Thanks, hon." She glanced back at Grady, but his attention was elsewhere. She followed his gaze, and saw a tiny woman, dressed in jeans and a tight black tank top, step in the door with a young girl about Jenna's age.

Terese Balfour, Claire realized. Had Grady arranged to meet her here? That would explain the way he'd been casing the joint.

Yes. Terese smiled and waved as she caught his gaze and Claire was surprised to see Grady flush in response.

"Excuse me a minute?" he asked her.

"Sure."

She watched him approach the counter and bend low to say something quietly to Terese, then to her young daughter. The little girl giggled and wrapped her arms around his waist.

Claire decided she should go outside and join her girls. She'd met Terese before; Terese had even been at the cottage for Drew and Mallory's wedding. But for some reason Claire didn't feel like saying hi.

SATURDAY, CLAIRE WAS cleaning the breakfast dishes when she heard Kirk's sedan pull up the lane. She glanced out the kitchen window, surprised to see him so early. The girls exploded out the front door before he had a chance to slide out from the front seat of his car.

"Daddy, Daddy! I lost my tooth!"

Claire moved away from the open window as

bittersweet pain brought yet more tears to her eyes. The girls loved him so much. Did he realize how lucky he was to have that special trust?

She went to the deck to gather the beach towels she'd put out on the railing to dry last night. Carefully, she folded them in a stack on a chair, then waited for the sound of the screen door closing, before she went back inside.

The three girls were trailing their father. Jenna was insisting that he check to see if *her* tooth was ready to come out, like Daisy's.

"Still going to be a while, kiddo," he told her.

It was nice to see Kirk out of business attire, wearing tan-colored shorts and a forest-green golf shirt. His dark blond hair had reddish glints in the bright morning light, and Claire could tell from across the room that he hadn't shaved.

The way the girls were clinging to him, you'd think they hadn't seen him in a month. Oddly enough, after all her talk of missing her father, Andie was the one who was hanging back. With a start, Claire realized her daughter was watching *her*.

Self-consciously, Claire crossed the room. "How was the drive?" All too aware of Andie's scrutiny, she leaned forward to kiss Kirk lightly on the cheek.

She saw the surprise flash in his eyes, then comprehension as he kissed her back, his hand reaching out to grasp her upper arm tightly.

"How are you, Claire?"

His question made her think of her pregnancy, and she was glad she'd worn her loose denim jumper—a perfect choice for camouflaging the changes to her body.

"Oh, the girls are trying to drive me crazy, as usual," she said, hugging Jenna and Daisy next to her. "But so far I've stayed out of the loony bin."

"Mo-om," Andie groaned. She sidled up to her father. "We're making strawberry shortcake for dessert tonight, Dad."

"Yum. My favorite." Kirk set his duffel bag and bulging briefcase on the floor.

"Can we go out on the boat this weekend?" Daisy asked him.

"Will you take us for an ice cream?"

"Yes and yes." Kirk nodded at the two youngest. "What about you, Andie? What's on your list for the weekend?"

Andie scuffed a sandaled foot against the pine floor.

"I'd like to do something as a family," she said. "Do you think we could all play Monopoly tonight?"

Claire pressed her lips together, aware that Kirk was checking her expression, but not daring to return his look. She nodded slightly, then heard him say, "Sure, Andie. If that's what you want."

"Does it have to be Monopoly, Andie?" Claire said, trying to sound lighthearted. "You know your father always wins when we play that game."

Family time she could handle, she decided. As long as she and Kirk didn't have to be alone.

It turned out there was no need to worry. The girls clung to his side all day.

First, they went for a cruise on the lake, taking along a picnic lunch, which they ate in the boat. Then Kirk drove the girls into town, giving her a chance to have a bit of a break.

Not that she was able to relax. To have Kirk here, to be acting as though they were one big happy family when the truth was just the opposite, was so bizarre. How long could they keep up this charade for the sake of the children?

And yet, a part of her was happy to see him. That she should feel this way, when he'd betrayed her as he had, struck her as so unfair. Why couldn't she just hate him and be done with it? That would be much simpler.

But she didn't hate Kirk. In fact, a tenderness swelled up in her, at the oddest moments. Such as when Daisy climbed on his lap to tell him about the new game she'd made up with her sisters. Or when he stopped in his tracks to fix a board that had come loose on the deck.

Not until late that night, past ten o'clock, after a dinner of barbecued hamburgers, with strawberry shortcake for dessert, and a two-hour-long game of Monopoly that finally ended in a stalemate between Andie and Kirk, did they have time to talk at last, just the two of them.

Not that Claire wanted to talk. But clearly, they couldn't go on as they were.

When Kirk came back from tucking the girls in, she had a pot of decaf coffee ready.

"Thanks." Kirk took his mug, and out of habit they went to sit by the fire—on opposite ends of the sofa. The night was uncharacteristically cool, and Kirk had built up a blaze while they were playing Monopoly. Now the logs glowed amber, giving them something to look at, rather than each other.

"The girls seem okay," Kirk finally said.

"Yes. Although Andie has had some ups and downs. I wish I knew what was going on in her head."

"I can't believe how her marks deteriorated this year."

"I still think there's a problem with the kids at school."

"Poor Andie."

Yes. Poor Andie. Claire felt like crying every time she imagined telling their eldest daughter they were getting a divorce. That was not what Andie needed right now. But maybe it would be better to get everything out in the open. Eventually, Andie would come to accept the situation—did she have any choice?

"We've got to tell them, Kirk."

Kirk rubbed his chin, and she heard the scratch of his whiskers. "What is it, exactly, that we're going to tell them?"

Was he being obtuse on purpose? "That we're separating." She wouldn't say *divorce,* not again. He would have to bring up the subject.

"Is that what we're doing?"

"Well, that's sure as hell how it feels." This was so frustrating. Why did he keep turning her questions around? She was trying to be realistic, trying to face the facts. Didn't he know how hard this was for her? Even when they were together, she felt as though a glass wall were separating them.

"You're the one who wanted me to move out," he reminded her. He finished his coffee and set the mug down on the table in front of them. "Have you given any further thought to the idea of counseling?"

How funny the way he asked that. As if she'd thought of anything else. The logical side of her knew it was a reasonable step to take. For the children's sake, if not hers and Kirk's. But the emotional side...

"Kirk, what's the chance we can save this marriage when you're in love with someone else?"

He had the grace to look abashed. "I've been doing a lot of thinking since you and the girls left." He leaned forward, staring into the fire.

"Oh?"

"I've missed you. All of you." He glanced at her, then turned away, as if he didn't really expect her to believe him. "If you agree to come to counseling with me, then I'll stop seeing Janice. I haven't seen her since you left, anyway."

Claire had to fight not to cry it was such a relief to find out he hadn't been spending all his time with Janice. Or had he? Could she really believe what he was telling her?

"How is that possible, when you work together?"

"I guess I should have been more clear. I've seen her at the office, but we haven't spoken. I told her I needed to sort things out with you first."

Oh, she wanted to believe him. But this man had lied to her in the past. He'd phoned to say he needed to work late, when it was really an excuse to spend time with Janice.

"And I should believe you because—"

Kirk's broad shoulders rose and fell on a long sigh. She could see the flush of color on his cheekbones, which were highlighted in the glow from the fire.

"I'll admit there were times when I stretched the truth—stretched it terribly. Usually, at least some work was involved." He sighed once more, then stood to throw another piece of birch on the fire.

"I guess there's more than one way to deceive your wife."

The color on his cheeks darkened. "Okay. I deserved that. The point is, Claire, I'm telling the truth now. I *am* making an effort to do the right thing. You believe I love my kids, don't you?"

Claire stood, crossing her arms over her chest. "Yes." She walked to the windows. In the dark the wall-length panes acted like mirrors. She tried to see past her image to the calm lake outside, but it was impossible.

Of course he loved his kids. But he didn't love her.

"Go ahead and book an appointment," she said. "Do you have a counselor in mind?"

He came up beside her, and for a moment she thought he would touch her, but he stayed a full arm's length away. "Yes. I phoned our family doctor. She gave me a name." He fished a card from his back pocket. "Riva Sharp. She specializes in family counseling, including couples therapy."

Couples therapy. To Claire the concept was suspect. She wondered how many of the couples who went to therapy ended up staying together. Or was this just an extra step to prolong the separation process?

"How about Tuesday afternoon?" Kirk asked. "Could you find someone to watch the girls?"

"I suppose you've already booked the appointment."

"Don't be angry, Claire. I hoped you'd say yes." He turned toward her then, touching her shoulder tentatively. "I can't stand living this way. I've got to know if we can fix our marriage."

Or not. Claire moved away from him, toward the fire. She wasn't sure if she wanted to beat him with her fists or beg him to hold her. Either way, to be near him wasn't safe. She picked up the poker and opened the screen. When she tried to flip over the remnant of the last log, it dissolved into ashes. She returned the poker to its cast-iron stand and shut the mesh screening.

"Okay," she said finally. "What time?"

"Two o'clock."

"I'll be there."

CHAPTER EIGHT

THE NEXT MORNING KIRK SPENT a couple of hours out on the deck after a long early-morning swim, dealing with that bulging briefcase he'd brought from the office. Claire sipped herbal tea until she shook off her dull headache—the legacy of yet another restless night.

She'd meant to tell Kirk yesterday that she was pregnant. Several times she'd even opened her mouth, but somehow the words had stalled at the back of her throat.

Why hadn't she told him?

Because it wasn't supposed to be this way! A new baby was supposed to be *good* news. Not a complication in an already volatile situation.

She didn't want to see Kirk's face crumple in resignation or shock or disbelief when he heard about this baby. Not after he'd been so delighted about the first three. She'd never forget how tightly he'd squeezed her when they got the call about Andie. Or how he'd sent flowers when she was just six weeks pregnant with Daisy—giving Claire the inspiration for her second daughter's name. Two years later, when her third pregnancy was confirmed, they'd splurged on a sitter to go out for dinner.

Their financial situation had been tighter back then. That dinner out had been a real treat. Odd how, now that they could afford it, she couldn't remember the last time she and Kirk had gone out just the two of them.

Why had it taken Kirk's confession to make her notice these things? The dwindling of loving words and actions, of time spent together. The thoughtful touches that had made them a couple, not just mother and father to the same three kids.

The changes had taken place so gradually she'd never realized her marriage had entered the danger zone.

Claire rinsed out her mug and placed it in the dishwasher. The girls were outside collecting items from a scavenger list she'd given them after breakfast. First one to come up with all twelve would get the plastic figure they'd found in the bottom of the cereal box that morning. In the meantime, she wanted to experiment with some recipes for this week's column. She had an idea for a fat-reduced potato salad. And her bean-and-corn salad with cilantro was always a big hit. Once made, she could serve them as an early dinner, before Kirk went back to Toronto.

Claire didn't know whether she was relieved or

disappointed about his upcoming departure. Of course, it wouldn't be long until she saw him again.

They had that appointment booked for Tuesday. Just thinking about it made her belly tighten with apprehension. Did Kirk really want to salvage their marriage? Or was he just going through the motions so he could tell himself he'd done everything he could to try to make it work?

Or maybe he was doing it for their children. Because, like her, he hated to break up their comfortable, secure home.

That wasn't a bad reason, of course, but as she scrubbed potatoes with a vegetable brush, Claire had to admit that she wished he were motivated by more than good intentions toward his family.

Where did his feelings for her factor in? she mused. If indeed he had any.

AT NOON ON TUESDAY, Claire dropped her children off at Mallory's. They were excited at the prospect of spending the day in Port Carling with Angel. Mallory was going to take them down to the park by the bridge, where they could watch the motorboats traveling through the locks between Lakes Muskoka and Rosseau. If they were lucky, they'd spot the RMS *Segwun* as the steamship passed through the locks or stopped for passengers.

''Here's a batch of granola squares for the kids

to snack on." Claire set the plastic container on Mallory's kitchen counter. "And this bag has spare clothing, suntan lotion and hats."

"Perfect." Mallory leaned against the counter, munching on an apple. "You're always so organized. With three children, how do you do it?"

"With three children, how could I not?" Claire opened her purse and pulled out a couple of sheets of paper. "I also have my column for the *Gazette*. Could you give it to Drew for me?"

"You bet." Mallory took the envelope. "Drew says he's had lots of calls about your first column."

"Oh?" Claire had wondered if there would be any reaction.

"All positive. I guess a lot of people have missed that column these past few years."

"Well, that's a relief. It isn't easy following in the footsteps of Angela Driscoll."

"I know. She really was something. Drew and I still miss her so much."

Claire squeezed her friend's shoulder. Angie's cancer had struck her down so swiftly her family and friends had had no time to prepare for the loss.

"She would have been so happy to see you and Drew together. And Angel..."

"I like to think so."

"By the way, did you try the recipe? The strawberry shortcake?"

"Claire, you know Drew and I are culinary challenged. We rely on you for our home-cooked meals. But I heard Grady had a lot of success with the recipe this weekend. The twins dropped off their sports column last night and mentioned that he'd served the shortcake for dessert."

Had Terese and her daughter been there to share it? Claire didn't ask the question because she was ashamed of the stab of resentment she felt at the thought of the young mother and her child enjoying a meal with the Hogans.

She didn't know why she wasn't pleased to see Grady in this new relationship. He certainly deserved to find his own happiness now that Bess had left. And while Claire had reservations about Terese, obviously everyone else liked her.

"I don't mean to rush you," Mallory said, "but shouldn't you be going? You said your appointment was at two."

Claire's stomach tensed around the bran muffin and milk she'd forced herself to have for breakfast. Glancing down at her watch, she nodded. "You're right. Wish me luck."

Mallory walked her to the van, then leaned through the open window as Claire turned the key in the ignition. "I want nothing more than for you and Kirk to sort this out," she said. "And don't worry about the girls. We'll have lots of fun."

"You know, one thing this disaster has reminded me of is how lucky I am to have good friends like you and Drew." Claire slipped on her sunglasses. "Thanks, Mallory."

Mallory patted her arm. "You bet. Now, don't rush back. Take whatever time you need. And don't worry," she added in a louder voice as Claire pulled out from the curb.

Claire smiled and waved. *Don't worry.* How could she not?

The counselor Kirk had chosen was from Barrie. The city was a reasonable midpoint between the cottage and Toronto—indicative, perhaps, of the kind of compromise they'd need to save their marriage.

Save their marriage…

For a second, hope lightened the pressure against her chest, but all too soon realism set in. Regardless of whether Kirk had slept with Janice, he'd broken his wedding vow to Claire. He was in love with the other woman, and how could Claire compete? She was ten years older, overweight— and *pregnant* on top of everything!

And she didn't even want to compete. After twelve years, she shouldn't have to. If Kirk didn't value what they had together, then she didn't want him.

She turned the radio up loud and tried not to think as the miles flew by. Kirk had left her Riva Sharp's business card, and the address was easy to find. Claire eased the van into a parking spot in front of the small brick structure, which housed a legal firm and an insurance brokerage, as well as the counseling practice.

Kirk's sedan was already there, parked across the street, and she stared at it for a few seconds before pulling down the flap over the vanity mirror and reapplying her lipstick. What to wear to a marriage counseling session? That had been her quandary this morning. It had been complicated, of course, by her need to hide her pregnancy.

But hiding it would no longer be necessary after today. She was going to tell Kirk for sure this time. Maybe after the session was over they could go for a coffee or something.

If they were still speaking.

She flicked the switch to lock the van doors, then smoothed down her denim jumper. She was wearing a black, scooped-neck top underneath, and fashionable black platform sandals. Silver hoops hung from her ears, and her toenails gleamed rose-pink from last night's manicure.

She looked okay for a thirty-seven-year-old woman who was three months pregnant. And whose husband was in love with another woman.

RIVA SHARP'S OFFICE WAS both cozy and professional in appearance. The walls were lined with bookshelves and a desk was tucked discreetly behind an intimate arrangement of a sofa and several chairs.

Kirk was sitting in one of those chairs when Riva opened the door. Claire felt her heart thud at the sight of him. He looked so handsome, so calm and assured. How was that possible?

He was dressed in a navy four-button suit, with a pale blue shirt and one of his jazzier ties. Somehow she knew he hadn't procrastinated in front of the mirror, as she had, trying to decide what to wear.

Despite the fresh coat of lipstick, her lips felt dry as she smiled at him, before she turned to the counselor. Riva seemed to be in her early forties. Black hair streaked with silver, warm eyes like toasted pecans, and a wide smile. She was wearing a full-skirted cotton dress that swished around her legs as she walked. On her feet she had on Birkenstocks, her toenails unpainted.

"Come in, Claire. How was the drive? Would you like a coffee?"

"She takes cream," Kirk said.

Amused, Claire sat on the sofa, vaguely aware that Kirk had risen, then seated himself again. Two mugs already sat on ceramic coasters on the low table in front of them, next to a glass bowl of paper-wrapped candies. A moment later, a third mug was placed on a new coaster in front of her.

"There you go, Claire. I'm so glad you could make it."

How genial everyone was behaving, as if this were a simple social gathering. Claire set her purse in her lap and folded her arms over it. Riva took a chair on the other side of the sofa. If someone had drawn lines connecting the three of them, the result would have been an equilateral triangle. *Perfectly balanced,* Claire thought, *with no biases.* Another omen?

"So how are you doing, Claire?" Riva leaned forward over her thighs.

"I've been better." Now, there was an understatement.

"Yes. I'm sure you have. Kirk explained your situation to me over the phone. And we had a few minutes to talk before you arrived. Now it's your turn. Is there anything you'd like to ask me before we get started?"

"Does therapy really save marriages?" She hadn't meant to be so blunt, but wasn't that what she needed to know? She didn't want to go through weeks of meetings if there wasn't any hope.

"Therapy can help. It usually does." Riva sat back in her chair, her expression suddenly stern. "As for saving a marriage—well, that part's up to you. Up to both of you." She glanced at Kirk, then turned to Claire again.

"Do you want to save your marriage, Claire?"

The abrupt question caught her off guard. "I think Kirk should answer that first."

"Why?"

Wasn't it self-evident? Surely Kirk had told her the fundamentals of their situation. "He's the one who's fallen in love with someone else."

For the first time since she'd walked in the room, Claire angled her body so she faced her husband, and looked at him, really looked at him. He met her gaze with resignation. Or was it sorrow?

"Isn't that right?" she demanded, wanting him to say so out loud, in front of the therapist.

For a long moment he didn't answer. Then his chest rose with a deep, indrawn breath, and he nodded. "Janice and I had an emotional connection that Claire and I have been missing for a long time. That's true."

Jealousy, more potent than any venom, shot through Claire's bloodstream. Channeling the emotion into anger, she retaliated quickly. "Well, it's pretty hard to have an emotional connection with a man who's never home."

Kirk didn't defend himself, and in the ensuing silence, Riva spoke cautiously. "I understand your anger, Claire. But have you seen the positive aspect of this situation?"

"Positive aspect?" Up until this moment Claire had reserved judgment on the older woman. Now she had to wonder at Riva's sanity.

"What I'm getting at," the therapist continued, "is that Kirk told you about this woman before the relationship progressed to a fully intimate stage. That has to tell you something, Claire."

What the counselor wanted her to say was obvious. That Kirk's honesty was a sign he cared about the marriage. If they were talking about one incident only, Claire might be more prepared to agree. But Kirk had deceived her for months. He was an adult; he'd known what he was doing.

"It says he was feeling bloody guilty!"

She took a shallow breath, then continued. "As he should have. The fact that he didn't sleep with her doesn't make it any less wrong. He fell in love with her!"

Riva's expression was noncommittal. Didn't she get it?

"For months he told me lies, neglected our kids, spent all his free time with her. So what if they didn't actually have sex? And so what if guilt finally made him admit the truth to me? He should never have let the relationship progress as far as it did."

She was raving. Claire knew it, and she tried to calm down, but damn it, she felt the counselor was making excuses for Kirk.

"You may not think my husband's had an affair, and maybe technically he hasn't. But in his heart—'' she glanced at Kirk, meeting his gaze ''—he's as guilty as sin and he knows it.''

Kirk held her look; the only indications that he'd taken in her words were the paling of his complexion and the tightening of his lips.

After a few moments of silence, Riva finally spoke. "Do you have anything to say, Kirk?"

He cleared his throat and shifted his gaze from Claire to Riva. "She's right. I let my relationship with Janice stray out of bounds. And I knew what I was doing. I can't justify it, beyond saying that it made me happy to be with her."

No! Did he have any idea how that hurt?

"I can see that upsets you," Riva said quietly. "What's wrong, Claire?"

"*I'm* the one he's supposed to be happy with."

"But are you happy with me?" Kirk countered. "It doesn't feel that way. When I come home, all I sense from you is disappointment. I don't even have my foot in the door and I know you're already angry at me."

"There's a difference between my being angry when you come home late from work and your having an affair!"

Kirk's expression was cold as he replied, "I suppose there is."

He was unbelievable! Claire wanted to walk out of the room right then, but Riva leaned over and placed a hand on hers. "An affair doesn't have to mean the end of a marriage."

Claire thought about that for a minute. "You mean you get couples where one of the partners was actually sleeping with someone else and they end up staying together?"

"It happens all the time. More often than you might think. There are reasons, good reasons, for keeping a marriage together. At the same time, affairs do happen. Sometimes, the partners can get past it. Sometimes, they can't. Often, it depends on the basis for the marriage in the first place. Are the spouses well matched? Do they share values and interests?"

Once, Claire would have said yes to those questions. Now she thought about the hours Kirk put into work. He was consumed by his need for success. Had he consciously placed his work goals ahead of the needs of his wife and children?

"Kirk's job has come first for a long time now."

"That's not fair," he retaliated. "Just because I don't work nine to five doesn't mean I don't love my family."

"Doesn't it? When was the last time you went to one of the kids' soccer games? You couldn't make Daisy's dance recital in June."

"I couldn't help it that I had a meeting—"

Had he? Or maybe he'd just been spending more time with Janice. Claire wondered why was she sitting here. Listening to him was just making her more angry. More resentful. "There's always some excuse, isn't there."

"You don't appreciate the pressures of my job."

"And you don't appreciate the pressures of *mine*." He thought staying home and taking care of three kids was a picnic. She knew he did. "It would be nice to have a little assistance at times. It would be nice to have a break, occasionally, at the end of a day."

"I've told you I'd have no problem with you hiring a cleaning lady."

A cleaning lady? The man just didn't get it. "God, Kirk, I'm three months pregnant and you haven't been around enough to notice!"

CHAPTER NINE

"PREGNANT?" KIRK FELL BACK in his chair, the world around him darkening so that there was only one focal point. His wife's face.

She'd gone quiet. The poison in their argument had found its antidote, and that had been her stunning announcement.

"Pregnant." He knew it was true. Subtle signs he'd been too troubled to detect lined up like arrows marking the route on a map.

His gaze slid down the front of her denim dress, which couldn't quite disguise the thickening of her waist, the fullness of her breasts. In some corner of his brain he'd registered that his wife was gaining weight. It hadn't occurred to him to wonder why.

"You could have told me."

Claire looked at him wearily. "Could I have?"

Emotion squeezed off his throat. Blinking, Kirk stood, then groped his way to the window.

Could I have? Claire's question was still alive in the room, bouncing off the walls, playing over and over in his head.

Of course she couldn't have told him. She was right. He spent almost all his time at work, and when he *was* home, he was hardly accessible. At least not emotionally.

Kirk pressed his forehead against the cool glass of the window. God, what was the matter with him? How could he be in this mess? These past six months...at each step he'd felt somehow justified in what he was doing. Now, looking back, he felt only disgust. Disgust for the choices he'd made and the pain he'd caused. For all of them.

Claire, Janice and himself. There were no winners in this game. No matter what the eventual outcome, no one would emerge unscathed.

''Obviously Claire's revelation came as a shock to you, Kirk,'' Riva stated.

He nodded, returning to his chair but unable to look at Claire. Time—he needed some time. Claire's pregnancy changed everything, although how he wasn't sure. Did one unborn child count for more than three existing ones?

He thought of his daughters, and cords of guilt wrapped around his neck. Oh, God, what had he done? And how to go about setting things right? To find the right words took effort, and when he did, his voice wasn't as steady as he would have liked.

''I think the basics are there for Claire and me. But we've never had the marriage we ought to have had. If we're going to get anywhere, I think we both have to admit that much.''

Claire looked at him as if he'd betrayed her yet again.

But he couldn't back off. If he didn't finish now, it would never be said. ''Something's always been missing.''

''No.''

There it was. That blank denial. How could he argue when she refused to see their past for what it was?

''Why are we here?'' Claire's hands trembled. ''If you were never happy, why bother trying to fix things at this late stage?''

Despite his own bitter guilt he felt anger. Claire was never going to forgive him, let alone work on the problems that had wedged between them right from the start. Maybe it was time to give up.

Then he thought of the unborn baby, and his anger deepened. So he hadn't been around as much as he should have. Still, he hadn't deserved to find out about her pregnancy this way. Claire throwing the news at him as though it was her secret trump card. *Hah! Take that!*

Well, if causing him pain had been her goal, she'd sure as hell succeeded. But in terms of preserving their marriage...

He wondered if he was the only one who felt they were hardly moving in the right direction.

SOMEHOW Riva managed to dissipate their hostility enough to convince Claire and Kirk to book a second appointment. Claire left Kirk at the reception desk to settle their account.

On the street, she fished anxiously in her purse for her keys. Kirk's bitter analysis of their life together was all she could think of. So their relationship had always been flawed. Kirk had never been happy. That was what she'd driven all this way to discover. She should have known he'd blame everything on her. Never mind that *he'd* lied and cheated and fallen in love with someone new...

The door to the van was warm as she lifted the handle. Inside, the heated air was suffocating, and she flinched when she touched the hot vinyl of the steering wheel. After turning on the engine, she put the air conditioner on High, and that was when she spotted the slip of paper trapped beneath her windshield wiper.

Damn! A parking ticket. She hadn't even noticed the meter earlier.

She climbed out of the van and was just lifting the wiper blade when Kirk came out of the office. She stuffed the ticket into the side pocket of her jumper, then got back into the van. But not fast enough.

"Where the hell do you think you're going?"

The anger in his voice, the actual words he used

made her heart pound. Kirk didn't normally talk that way. She pressed a button on the panel by her elbow, and the passenger window opened smoothly.

"Don't swear at me!"

Ignoring the open window, he yanked at the passenger door, then hauled his body into the seat next to her. The van was roomy, but Claire still felt uncomfortable, aware that they hadn't sat this close in the therapist's office. She tried to ignore him as she adjusted the vent so it was blowing cool air directly at her face.

"Don't you think we ought to talk?"

He sounded calmer now, but she was still annoyed. "It didn't seem to do us much good in there."

Kirk twisted in his seat until he was facing her, his gaze steady. "Hell of a way to find out my wife is pregnant. Couldn't you have told me this weekend?"

She gripped the wheel and stared ahead of her. "Maybe I would have. If I'd felt more like a wife and less like unwanted baggage."

"Unwanted baggage," he repeated bitterly. "That pretty much sums it up, doesn't it?"

What did he mean? Was that really how he saw her? She didn't have the nerve to ask.

"Three months, Claire? Are you really that far along?"

She glanced sideways and saw him eyeing her stomach, her breasts. With her seat belt fastened, the signs were all too obvious.

"Yes. I went to the doctor a few days before you told me about—about Janice. I'd just got off the phone with the results when you came into the kitchen."

He cursed. "Great timing."

Claire swallowed, thinking about the child she was carrying. The poor thing couldn't help that its parents were in such a muddle. Yet it would surely have to live with the consequences.

"But why did you go to the doctor so late? With the others we knew by six weeks."

"I don't know why I didn't notice the signs. I guess I lost track of my period...." Claire trailed off as she wondered if she was just kidding herself. Had she really been so oblivious to the messages her body was giving her? True, she didn't get the morning sickness that so many other women suffered from, but she'd been tired and her breasts had swollen. Then there'd been the missed periods.

Maybe she'd ignored the signals because subconsciously she'd known her marriage was in trouble.

"This shock, all the unhappiness..." Kirk shook his head. "I know you haven't been eating that well. Or sleeping, either. Have you talked to your doctor about possible impact on the baby?"

"My next appointment isn't for three weeks. I saw the doctor just before we left for the lake. At that point I'd lost some weight—but that's typical for the first trimester." She thought of the tests he'd suggested—she was over thirty-five now, and there were precautions that should be taken. But this wasn't the time for that discussion.

"You never lost any weight with the first three."

True. It wasn't the pregnancy; it was the emotional duress, and her resulting lack of appetite, that was to blame. "I'm *trying* to eat properly."

"Oh, Claire." Kirk touched the side of her cheek with his hand.

For a moment Claire closed her eyes, the caress of Kirk's hand all she cared to think about. Underneath the polished businessman veneer, Kirk had a tender side that she'd seen too little of lately. Except when he was with the girls. He had inordinate patience with them sometimes, she thought, even more than she did.

"How did this happen to us?" he asked.

Claire's eyes opened at the reminder of their situation. "How did this happen?" She pulled back from his touch and slipped her sunglasses from the visor. "I'm not the one who needs to answer that question."

So much for the tenderness in Kirk's expression.

He leaned back in his chair, his mouth thinned to a hard, tight line.

She stared at him pointedly. "I have to go, Kirk. Mallory's got the girls and I promised I'd be home before dinner." Actually, she hadn't said when she'd be home. And hadn't Mallory told her not to rush back? But Kirk didn't know any of that.

"I want to come out this weekend. Friday night, if that's okay."

It wasn't okay. She didn't want to face up to what was happening between them. She didn't want to analyze what had gone wrong or figure out how to set things right. Now all she felt was anger, and concentrating on that seemed easier.

But then she thought of the girls' disappointment if their father didn't come for the weekend.

"Yes," she said, fixing her eyes on the road in front of her. "The girls would like that."

"The girls, Claire?"

She knew what he was asking, of course, and it was definitely too much.

"I have to go," she repeated.

He looked at her a full minute, but she refused to meet his gaze, focusing, instead, on the street, on the dotted white line, on the traffic lights where she had to turn to meet the highway. Finally, he let out a ragged sigh. "Okay, then."

He opened the passenger door and stepped out

onto the sidewalk. "You will take care of yourself?
Eat properly and get enough sleep?"

His concern for his unborn child was touching.
When it had been just *her,* he hadn't worried so.
She nodded curtly, still staring out the front win-
dow, and waited for him to close the door.

"It's not just the baby I'm worried about."

Oh, sure. As though she were fool enough to
believe that. "I'll be careful, Kirk."

"Good. I'll see you Friday."

CHAPTER TEN

HOLDING HERSELF TOGETHER for the rest of that week wasn't easy, but somehow Claire managed. She had to, because of the children.

Thank goodness she had them. If not, she might have gone insane, or driven off in the van and never come back. All thoughts of Kirk, of their twelve-year marriage, brought with them lashes of pain. Yet she could think of little else.

She wondered where they had gone wrong, why Kirk hadn't talked to her, why he had turned to Janice.

And most painful of all, Claire wondered if he was missing Janice now. He'd said he wouldn't see her while he and Claire were going to their counseling sessions. But did he want to? Was he still thinking of the other woman? Dreaming of her?

When Grady invited Claire and the girls to go waterskiing late Thursday afternoon, Claire accepted eagerly. The distraction was badly needed. Not just by her, but by the girls. All day Wednesday, and this morning, too, they'd been at one another's throats. Especially Andie and Daisy.

Now, ensconced in Grady's sixteen-foot fiber-glass runabout, Claire took her first full relaxing breath of the day. She sat sideways so she could keep an eye on Andie, who was skiing behind the wake, a proud smile spread over her face. Daisy and Jenna sat in the two back seats, waving madly at their elder sister.

"She's doing great," Grady shouted after a glance over his shoulder. Then he grinned at Claire and winked. She focused briefly on his rugged face, the white flash of his teeth, the breadth of his shoulders.

Grady was a big man—well over six feet, with a husky build. Although the summer season had just begun, he was already tanned. Her eye followed the tapered line that led from his bare chest to his flat belly. And he was clearly in shape.

Self-consciously, she tugged the white T-shirt she wore over her suit, a maternity model built to accommodate her expanding waistline. She herself wouldn't be drawing any admiring looks this summer. Not that she had in years. Somehow those five extra pounds hadn't disappeared after Jenna the way they had with the other two.

What would happen after this one? Would she gain even more weight? Ten pounds instead of five? It didn't bear thinking about. Pressing her sunglasses up against the bridge of her nose, she turned her attention back to Andie, who was still skimming over the lake.

"Way to go, Andie!" Claire waved encouragingly. Too bad Kirk had to miss this—their eldest daughter's first ski of the season. The thought came automatically, followed quickly by a stab of pain. Kirk wasn't here, and maybe, after this summer, he would never be again. At least not when she was around.

Claire swallowed, and jabbed at her sunglasses again. She could see the Hogans' gray-painted dock in front of them. Grady's son Taylor was standing at the edge, shouting instructions to Andie. Beside him were two other people who hadn't been there earlier. A woman and a child. Terese Balfour and her daughter, Lisa.

Claire glanced at Grady. He, too, had spotted the newcomers and had his hand raised in welcome. Claire swallowed and turned back toward Andie. They were close to the dock. It was almost time for Andie to let go of the rope...

"Now, Andie!"

At Taylor's signal, Andie dropped the handle, and the rope skidded ahead without her. For a moment she seemed to be standing on water, then slowly she began to sink into the lake.

"Oh! It's cold!" Claire heard her daughter call out as Grady swung the boat around.

"Good work, Andie!" Taylor positioned himself on the dock, then dived in to help retrieve the skis while Andie swam ashore.

Terese, her tiny body looking terrific in a black bikini, her olive-toned skin almost as bronzed as Grady's, leaned over to offer her a hand. "Well done!"

"Hey, Terese! Glad you could make it. Would Lisa like to ride in the boat?"

"I have my life jacket on," Lisa pointed out, tugging on Terese's hand. The five-year-old had her mother's dark coloring, but her hair was longer, and currently tied back in two high pigtails. "Can I ski?"

"Not this year," Terese said. "Maybe later Grady will pull you and the other girls behind the boat in a tube."

"How about you, Terese?" Grady asked, sliding his sunglasses up on his head. "Would you like to have a go?"

When the other woman nodded, Claire faced Grady.

"Has she skied before?"

"A few times."

Half expecting the younger woman to fall flat on her face, Claire was surprised when Terese popped out of the water on the first try. Although obviously a beginner, she managed to break out from behind the wake to cut a few turns, before Grady headed back to the dock.

Terese swam directly for the boat when she'd finished her attempt. Laughing, she let Grady pull her out of the water. Claire averted her eyes rather than see Terese's flat belly.

For a woman to look that good, especially when she'd had a baby, wasn't fair. And it especially wasn't fair that Grady so obviously noticed. He wrapped a towel around Terese's soaked body and asked Jenna if she could share her seat.

Claire decided to sit out on the dock while first Taylor, then Grady went for a spin. Both were incredible skiers, but after several long runs it was clear that Taylor had finally surpassed his father in endurance, if nothing else.

"Whew!" Grady pulled himself out of the water and flopped down on the stained cedar dock next to Claire while he caught his breath. "I hate to admit it, but I can't keep up with that boy anymore."

At the wheel, Taylor called out to his father, "I'm going to take the girls tubing. Is that okay? Andie can spot for me."

Grady glanced at Claire and, when she nodded, called back, "Okay, son."

Terese helped settle Daisy, Jenna and Lisa inside the large rubber tube, then pushed away from the boat and swam toward shore. Taylor started the boat moving, and all three girls shrieked with pleasure.

For a moment, Claire watched vigilantly. Satisfied that everyone was safe, she rested her face on bent knees and turned to Grady, who had dried off with a small white towel that now hung around his neck. His attention was focused on Terese, who was still swimming back to the dock.

"Happy, Grady?" Claire asked.

He glanced sideways at her, then back to the boat, which was cutting a wide circle on the lake.

"Amazingly enough, yes," he said at last. "The divorce hasn't been easy, but I think I've finally put it behind me."

"I'm glad." Claire didn't think she'd ever understand how Bess could have left Grady. Grady was someone a woman could count on. He'd married Bess when she'd told him she was pregnant. Claire was willing to bet *he'd* never cheated during their years of marriage. And the divorce—that had almost killed him, but he'd never said a word against Bess. Still didn't.

"You and Terese..." She deliberately left the sentence unfinished, hoping he'd tell her about their relationship.

But Grady just smiled.

A moment later, Terese was within earshot. Grady crouched low and offered her a hand as her feet sought purchase on the metal ladder.

"Hi, Claire," she said, slightly out of breath. "Your girls are sure having a blast."

"Yes." There was warmth in Terese's almond-shaped eyes, but Claire had never felt comfortable in her presence and didn't feel comfortable now.

Was it due to Terese that Grady had finally made peace with his divorce from Bess? If that was true, then Claire knew she ought to feel thankful. But for some reason, that wasn't the way she felt at all.

Mallory and Drew both thought Terese was great, but that didn't mean she was the right woman for Grady. After all, she came with a lot of baggage. Not the least of which was an abusive ex-husband and a young daughter.

Was she really the best choice for Grady? Somehow Claire didn't think so.

CLAIRE WAS LYING on her bed Friday night when she heard Kirk's sedan in the driveway. The numbers on the bedside alarm clock glowed red in the dark: 11:05. He'd phoned while she and the girls were eating beans and wieners on the deck and said he'd be a little late.

Why? What are you doing? Who are you with?

She hadn't asked any of those questions, although she'd been tempted. Now she rolled onto her side as she heard him open the door, drop his keys on the counter, set his bag on the floor. How many times had she lain in bed listening for those familiar sounds?

She heard his footsteps in the hall, then the

sound of doors opening and closing as he checked on the girls—Daisy and Andie in the bunk beds, Jenna in the double bed next door. Shutting her eyes, Claire imagined what he saw. Young bodies tangled in bedclothes, smelling of lake water and sunscreen despite vigorous scrubbing in the shower earlier. Hair splayed on pillows, noses freckled, eyelashes resting on smooth white cheeks. Books and stuffed animals scattered on the floor. Jenna's new rock collection in a pail by her bed.

Claire realized she was stroking her tummy. Next summer there would be one more bed—a crib—and one more tiny face to kiss good-night.

Now the footsteps paused and Claire knew Kirk was standing by her door. Would he push the door open, or go sleep on the couch? She'd left an extra pillow plus an old afghan on one of the cushions. Just as she'd done last weekend.

She took a deep breath, thinking of the times before, how her being pregnant had seemed to turn Kirk on. While other expecting women complained that their husbands treated them as if they had an infectious disease, Kirk had wanted to make love more often than usual. He'd relished cupping her swollen breasts in his hands, covering her growing belly in soft, warm kisses.

They'd been a little nervous with their first child, until her doctor had reassured them that if Claire felt no discomfort, then the baby would be fine.

Claire had felt a lot of things, but discomfort wasn't one of them. Now the familiar tingling sensation stirred in her, traveling from the tips of her breasts to the warmth between her legs. She missed making love. How long had it been now? Claire did some quick arithmetic and arrived at a total of just over five weeks. If they were getting a divorce, then this was another one of the adjustments she would have to make.

But maybe they would survive this crisis. The words of the counselor came back to her, as they so often had since Tuesday.

An affair doesn't have to mean the end of a marriage.

Was it true? Claire wondered if there were couples in her own circle of friends who had gone through similar situations. If so, it was something they didn't talk about.

Sinking into her pillow, she tried to remember the good things about her marriage, back in the early days. Surely sex had been one of them. At least from what she remembered.

A similar sense of humor had been another. Laughing together was something they hadn't done for even longer than making love.

And talking until the wee hours of the night. When she'd first met Kirk there had never seemed to be enough time to say all that was in her mind. Now they only communicated about the children.

"Kirk?" She stepped out onto the cool plank floor and reached for her thin cotton wrap just as the door swung open. There were no curtains on the open window, and pale light from the moon made it possible for her to see the dark silhouette of his body. Tall, lean, broad shouldered...

"Sorry. Did I wake you?"

He'd been standing behind her closed door for almost five minutes. What had he been thinking?

"No. I was feeling kind of restless."

"Can I make you some herbal tea?"

"That would be nice." She followed him to the kitchen, where he turned on the light over the stove. He was still wearing his suit from the office, although he'd removed his tie and loosened the top buttons of his shirt. His hair had grown a little, and one of the curls fell over his forehead.

Now he brushed it back with his hand before taking the bottled water from the fridge and filling the kettle.

"I wish I could have been here before the kids went to bed, but I had some paperwork to catch up on." He glanced at her, as if expecting her to question him further, but she just slid onto a stool and leaned her elbows on the counter.

"You should have seen Andie when she stood up on skis yesterday. She was so nervous at first, then she got this grin on her face."

"I can imagine. She sounded thrilled when she

told me on the phone. I'm sorry I missed it.'' He put tea bags into mugs. ''Do you think Grady would take us out on the boat this weekend? I'd love to see Daisy try for her first time.''

''I'm sure he would, but I don't know if Daisy's ready. She looked pretty nervous when Andie was skiing.''

''Well, we won't rush her.'' Kirk poured the boiling water into the mugs.

Watching Kirk perform the simple domestic task, Claire realized they were talking about the kids again. Maybe it was no wonder their marriage had fallen apart.

''What do you say we drink these on the deck.''

''Sure.'' She followed him out the sliding doors, noticing the way he paused slightly at the sofa. Maybe he'd seen the pillow and the blanket and drawn the obvious conclusion.

It was warm outside—too warm, really. She felt sticky and flushed even in her nightie and wrap, which were made of the thinnest cotton and only came down to midthigh. At least there was a breeze. She stood at the railing, admiring the trail of moonlight on the gently rippled surface of the lake.

''Did you hear that?'' Kirk asked, handing her one of the mugs. ''Careful, it's hot.''

She balanced the mug on the cedar railing and tilted her head to listen. ''An owl?''

"I love that sound. It always reminds me of the first time you brought me here. Remember how we sneaked out in the canoe once your parents were asleep?"

Claire laughed softly. They'd paddled out from shore, then made love awkwardly but passionately on a quilted blanket Kirk had spread on the wooden floor between the seats. An owl had skimmed across the sky, so close they heard the rustle of his feathers an instant before his unearthly call had punctuated the crucial moment.

"That was unforgettable," she agreed. A pressure on her arm made her glance down to where Kirk had placed his hand.

"You look beautiful, Claire. You're so lovely when you're pregnant."

She hadn't realized he was staring at her, and now the intensity of his expression had her catching her breath. "You couldn't even tell I was expecting the last time you saw me," she reminded him. Only four days ago. She wouldn't have changed much in that amount of time.

"I must have been blind not to have noticed." His eyes traveled down from her face to the low scoop of her nightie, then to the thin fabric that clung to her breasts. She saw him moisten his lips, then gaze lower.

"May I?"

She didn't know what she was giving him permission to do, but when she nodded, he placed his other hand on her belly. She felt a responding stir between her legs and almost, but not quite, leaned into him.

"Hey, there, little one," he said softly. "This is your daddy talking."

That her eyes filled with tears at such a simple comment seemed silly, but they did. Kirk had always liked to talk as if the unborn baby could hear him.

"Don't you worry," he continued. "Your mama and I are going to take care of you." He looked back at her, his expression fierce. "No matter what happens. Aren't we, Claire?"

She nodded again, not trusting her voice.

"And I'm going to take care of you, too, Claire." He tipped her chin up and stared into her eyes until, Lord help her, she almost believed him.

"Are you, Kirk?" She was so tempted to beg him to be the husband and father that she and the girls needed.

But why? Did she still love Kirk? Despite his devotion to the office, his near affair with Janice? Or was it because she was pregnant and needed someone she could depend on?

Truth was, she didn't want to be a single mother with four children. But that wasn't reason enough to cling to a marriage that didn't work on other levels.

Still, the way she felt when he touched her—that had nothing to do with the children.

"I'm so confused..."

"Sit down, Claire." Kirk pulled over one of the wooden chairs. Once she was seated, he handed her her mug, then drew up a chair beside her.

"I'm sorry I've screwed up our lives this way."

"If only you'd come to me about the problems in our marriage before you turned to—"

"I know." He leaned forward on his knees, glancing sideways at her. "But it happened so gradually. I didn't realize what was missing in our marriage until I found it—with her."

That hurt. That really hurt. Claire sipped her tea, wishing she could recapture the warm, peaceful feeling she usually had when she sat out by the lake in the evening. Instead, she felt anxious and tense. And, yes, jealous.

Another woman had given Kirk the emotional intimacy that he should have been getting from her. That they should have been sharing together. Thinking of the two of them alone together, all those months, made her physically ill. And she'd never guessed....

"Did you see Janice at work this week?"

"She's on holiday...visiting her folks on Vancouver Island for a couple of weeks."

Good. If only she'd stay there. But Claire knew the solution would not be that simple.

Less than a foot away from her, her husband

cupped his mug and stared out across the lake. "It's over between Janice and me. You don't have to worry about that."

Claire sighed. "And I guess I'm supposed to take your word?"

"For what it's worth," he said. He stood abruptly and went to the sliding doors. "I take it I get the couch?"

"That was my plan. Although I could share Jenna's bed—"

"Let's leave the kids out of this for now."

"I'd love to do just that. But let's face it. As innocent as they are, our children are at the very heart of this situation. Whatever we decide will affect them for all their lives."

Kirk looked bleak as he turned back to face her. "Don't you think I know that? Don't you think I worry about that every minute of every day?"

Well, you didn't worry about it when you were having those late-night dinners with Janice! Claire bit back the angry words. What was the point in escalating their argument at this time of night?

"Why don't you go to bed, Claire. You need your rest."

As if she'd be able to fall asleep now. Still, Claire grabbed her mug and followed him indoors. She poured her tea down the drain—she'd only managed to swallow a few mouthfuls.

Not that it mattered. No amount of chamomile was going to bring her comfort tonight.

CHAPTER ELEVEN

THE COTTAGE WAS suspiciously quiet the next morning. From behind closed eyelids, Claire sensed another sunny day, and judging from the heat in the room, it was later than usual. Oh, joy of joys, maybe the girls had slept in.

She yawned and stretched, and her hand hit something solid. She pulled the paperback mystery she'd been reading last night out from under her pillow. She must have dozed off around chapter seven, she thought. Just when they'd determined the death wasn't accidental.

But if she'd fallen asleep reading, the light ought to be on. And it didn't seem right that the children could have slept this late. The small clock by the lamp claimed it was after ten—which the high angle of the sun's rays passing through the window verified.

Claire stretched again, and wondered how Kirk had fared on the sofa. Her stomach tightened the way it always did when she thought of her husband and the problems between them.

That was when she saw the tray on the bureau against the opposite wall.

She sat up and swung her feet onto the cool floor. Wilted dandelions hung their heads over a small glass vase. A note lay propped against the white thermos she'd normally used on the boat. Next to the thermos stood a mug and a cellophane-wrapped muffin.

She read the note: "Enjoy your breakfast in bed." The printing looked like Daisy's. The accompanying picture was Jenna's trademark rainbow.

Claire twisted the top off the thermos. Out seeped the aroma of Earl Grey tea. For a second she looked at the door. It was so darn quiet out there. Where were those kids? Where was Kirk?

Then she glanced back at the book on her pillow.

What the heck. She deserved a break, didn't she? Claire lifted the tray, then set it on the unoccupied half of the bed. She poured out a mugful of the tea, unwrapped the muffin and opened her book. Pulling up the pillow against the headboard, she settled herself back under the covers.

The brother had killed him, Claire decided. She was all but positive....

MAN, IT WAS HOT!

Kirk checked to see if Andie was still wearing

her hat. She had the pale skin of a true redhead: sunscreen alone didn't offer her enough protection.

There she was, at the far corner of the beach, sprawled out in the sand, reading one of the books he'd bought for her, the brim of her denim hat pulled low over her face.

Andie. Something was going on with that kid. He wasn't sure what. Daisy and Jenna had opened their arms for big hugs when he'd woken them with a finger to his lips for them to be quiet. But Andie had held herself aloof, her expression blank when he explained he wanted to give their mother a break this morning.

The two younger girls had helped him put the tray together. It was seven-thirty when he'd set it on Claire's bureau and turned out the light by her head. He'd never seen someone look sad in their sleep before, but that was exactly how Claire had looked to him with her flaxen hair spilled over the pillow, thin lines traced across her brow and down either side of her lips.

Sad and vulnerable. He'd felt a piercing guilt knowing he was the reason she looked that way, and he'd been so tempted to lie down next to her and smooth away those worry lines with soft touches and even softer words. But he'd known Claire wouldn't welcome him in her bed. And the girls were expecting him to keep them amused.

So he'd allowed himself merely to stroke the

side of her cheek before rounding up the girls and taking them to the Conroys' summer place just a few miles farther along the shore of Lake Rosseau.

Beaches were rare in Muskoka cottage country. Generally, the lakes butted up to solid rock, and most cottagers built long wooden docks connecting land and water.

Buddy and Pat Conroy's property was different. They'd bought the small cottage as an enticement to their children—who were now married, with children of their own—in the hope that Robert and Laura would spend more of their summer holidays with them.

Now that he was semiretired from his law practice, Buddy kept the small natural beach well groomed, and was always generous about sharing access with other friends from Port Carling. Especially those with small children.

"Let's build another sand castle, Daddy," Jenna said, tugging his arm.

The heat had made him somnolent, but he shook off his fatigue and padded along the sand to the water's edge. There Jenna handed him a bucket, with strict instructions on the type of sand he was to use.

"Not too wet, Daddy, or it mushes down. And not too dry or it won't stick."

"I've got it," he assured her. Crouching to his knees, he began to shovel. Lord but he was tired.

The couch was not the most comfortable place to sleep, especially since it was about six inches shorter than he was. 'Course, it seemed just fine when he was taking a lazy afternoon nap.

He might as well admit it. The situation between him and Claire had kept him up. That and the faint line of light he'd seen under her bedroom door.

Knowing she couldn't sleep, either, had caused him to feel guilty as hell. After all, she was pregnant. She *needed* her rest.

"Put it here, Daddy," Jenna commanded with all the authority of an office manager. Funny, you'd think that being the youngest, she'd be more used to *taking* orders than *giving* them. But right from the start Jenna had seemed to have more confidence than the other two.

Which made him wonder what this fourth child would be like.

He dumped the pail of sand in the area that Jenna had cleared, and was told to go get another. Obediently, he walked back to the water's edge. Daisy was wading at knee level, trying to catch something in a green plastic strainer.

"What're you looking for, Day?"

"Bugs."

She sounded so matter-of-fact it made him smile.

"Why bugs?"

"So I can feed my grasshopper."

"Your grasshopper?"

"He's in the jar by the castle."

Kirk dropped off the fresh pail of sand with Jenna, then went to check. Sure enough, a gray grasshopper sat in the bottom of an old jam jar. The lid had several airholes that had been punched in with a nail.

Daisy came up beside him with several water bugs in the strainer. Water spiders? They all had spindly legs with tiny bodies. They wouldn't make much of a meal, he figured. Besides, didn't grasshoppers eat grass?

Daisy took the jar out of his hand and struggled to open the lid. "Mrs. Conroy gave me this when I went inside to use the bathroom. She said to say she was making sandwiches for lunch."

"Daisy!" That had been at least half an hour ago. "Why didn't you tell me sooner?"

His daughter shrugged. "I didn't think of it." Her hair had grown, he noticed, so that her bouncy blond curls now brushed her shoulders.

Kirk glanced toward the cottage. From the outside deck Buddy waved at him, and he noticed Patricia carrying a tray of glasses out from the house. After a quick check of all three girls, he bounded up the lawn to join them.

"I never meant for you to feed us, Pat," he said.

"I know, Kirk. It's our pleasure. We love your girls." She pushed her graying hair back from her face. "I just got off the phone with Mallory. She and Drew are bringing Angel over for lunch, too."

Buddy looked up from the crossword. "Angel?" A smile spread over his usually implacable features. "That's good. We haven't seen her in a while."

"All of seven days." Patricia smiled indulgently. "This will be a good opportunity for the girls to play together."

Mallory. Drew. Kirk's insides had lurched at the mention of Claire's old friends. Had his wife told them about their problems? He was almost certain she would have. Mallory and Drew, as well as Grady Hogan, were Claire's best friends. She'd known them all her life, from the summers she'd spent up here at the cottage.

If Claire had said anything about Janice, about the baby, they'd think he was dirt.

And they'd be right.

"I'll get the girls washed up for lunch," he said.

"No rush," Patricia told him. "Let them play a few minutes longer. Can I offer you something to drink? Buddy's having iced tea."

"That would be nice, Patricia. May I help?"

"No problem. I have everything right here." She poured from a frosted pitcher, then passed him a glass.

"I'd better go back down to the beach." He

could see Jenna and Daisy from here, but Andie was too far away.

"I'll call when it's ready," Patricia said.

Ice chinked against the plastic glass as Kirk walked slowly back to the sand. He sat on the edge of the beach and watched his children play. Andie was still reading, but Daisy and Jenna had joined forces and were now building the castle around the grasshopper.

How had he come to this—turned into the kind of man that he himself despised? Hadn't he sworn when his father had left his mother to marry an aerobics instructor from his father's downtown gym that he would never do something like that to his own wife and children?

Not that he equated Janice with the vacuous young woman who'd only stayed with his father for two years before cutting out with the executive partner of his father's law firm.

No, Janice was an intelligent, attractive woman who was interested in a genuine, long-term, full relationship. That was what had brought this whole situation to a head.

"I don't know about you, but I'm ready to take our relationship to the next level," she'd told him during one of their dinners. She'd placed her hand on his arm and leaned forward, revealing—intentionally or not, he had no idea—a glimpse of her firm, upright breasts.

He'd known what she'd meant, of course. Sleeping together. It was a tempting proposition, but one that made it impossible for him to ignore the reality of his marriage.

"Let me think about that," he'd said. He didn't want an adulterous affair. Janice didn't, either. But neither did he want to break up his family. How had he arrived at such a reprehensible situation?

His relationship with Janice had started innocently enough. Or had it? If he was honest, he had to admit that right from the start he'd seen that Janice was attracted to him.

And he'd felt flattered.

Janice thought he was handsome. She often complimented him on his physique and how well he dressed. She knew he was the highest-grossing broker in the office and went out of her way to tell him how impressed she was.

Whereas all Claire ever saw was a man who was never home on time and who didn't do enough to help out with the house and kids.

Not that that was any sort of excuse—

He turned at the sound of an approaching vehicle. Sure enough, there was Drew's Explorer. Standing, he brushed sand from his khaki shorts and shielded his eyes with one hand. Out stepped Mallory, then Drew, who opened the passenger door to get Angel from her car seat.

They were here. Time to face the music.

Kirk stepped forward to greet them.

"HOW WAS YOUR DAY, MOM?" Daisy asked, after showing Claire her new pet grasshopper. His name was Sam. He did not like green eggs and ham. He did not like water beetles, either. Or spiders or flies. All those dead insects lay in the jar with him, alongside a clump of grass.

"Did you have a nice break?"

"I did." Claire squeezed Daisy, inhaling the little-girl scent, enhanced by the aromas of lake water and sunscreen.

Actually, she'd been bored silly. She'd finished her book around two in the afternoon. She'd been right. The murderer *was* the brother. Then she'd spent a few hours in the kitchen, improvising some fresh-fruit salsas for her next "Cottage Cooking" column.

She hadn't been able to stop worrying about the children. Kirk had left a note that he'd taken them to the Conroys' beach. Would he remember hats and sunscreen? Would he make sure they had enough to drink? The heat could be dehydrating.

But they'd made it home just fine, with the girls displaying no ill effects that she could see. Now Kirk was on the deck, barbecuing the chicken breasts she'd marinated earlier. Jenna was helping, chirping like a bird just before sunrise. As for Andie... She'd given Claire a look that Claire could only describe as accusing, before holing up in her bedroom.

During dinner, Andie continued to be sullen, withdrawn.

"Aren't you hungry after your busy day?" Claire asked, passing a mixture of chopped strawberries and blueberries tossed in a light lime vinaigrette with some cilantro, which she'd thought might appeal to the children.

Andie shook her head, not looking up from her plate. "I hate those green things. I'm not eating that."

Claire glanced at Kirk. From his expression she could tell he had no more idea what was going on with their eldest daughter than she did.

"Have a little more chicken, then," Claire said. "You've hardly eaten anything."

Andie set her knife and fork on the plate. "Can I go to my room?"

Claire looked again at Kirk, who said reluctantly, "No snacks later, Andie."

"I know." She pushed against the table, and her chair legs scraped on the old pine floor. Neither Claire nor Kirk said a word about being more careful. As Claire watched her daughter trudge back to her room, the descriptive word that came to mind was *despondent*.

"Do you think she got too much sun?" she asked Kirk.

"She was wearing her hat the whole time. And I made sure she put on plenty of sunscreen."

After dinner, Kirk insisted Claire relax on the deck with her tea while he supervised showers for the girls and put them to bed. It was still warm outside, even though the sun had set. Kirk's voice, low and soothing, traveled faintly through the open patio doors. He was singing an old favorite of all the girls—a song about a woman who'd swallowed a fly.

Since he'd found out she was pregnant, Kirk had been pampering her like a princess. Claire wasn't certain how she felt about that. Sure it was nice, but who was he really concerned about? Her or the baby?

How about both? That was the fair answer. After all, he'd been as considerate during her other three pregnancies.

Maybe that was the solution. If she kept herself pregnant...

Very funny. Claire finished her tea and set the empty cup on the arm of her chair as she went to stand at the railing.

The half hour right after sunset was such a peaceful time of day. The lake rippled lazily; she could hear the water lapping on the rocks below. The strands of clouds hugging the horizon glimmered mauve and pink. Above them, set in the deep blue sky, she could see a few of the brighter stars and the saucy arch of a new moon.

Only when Kirk touched her arm did she realize she'd stopped hearing his voice murmuring in the background to the girls.

"Are they asleep?"

He nodded, removing his hand and staring out at the lake, too. "Do you have any idea what's eating Andie?"

"Not really. She's been a bear with her sisters this week. Is it adolescence?"

"At ten?"

"It does seem early." She thought of the ease with which she and her eldest daughter had always communicated before this year. "If there is something wrong, I can't understand why she won't speak to me. She always has in the past."

"Same here. I just tried to talk to her, but she gave me the same look I've been getting all day. As if she just found out I was an ax murderer. Not unlike the looks I got from Mallory and Drew during lunch, by the way."

Claire dipped her head so he wouldn't see her smile.

"Of course, I can't say I blame them." Kirk reached over and took one of her hands. The left hand. The one with her wedding band and the engagement ring he'd given her on a night much like this one. They'd been out in the canoe. It had been a few days after the owl incident.

Kirk twirled the rings, and she found herself focusing on the band he himself wore on the ring finger of his left hand.

"I've been such an idiot, Claire. Since you and the girls have been gone I've had a lot of time to think."

Think? Thinking could be good or it could be bad. What if he'd decided he wanted to be with Janice? Claire suddenly wanted to ask him to keep quiet. If this was more bad news, she didn't want to hear it. Not tonight. Not ever, to be honest.

But Kirk had something to say.

"I never should have let my friendship with Janice get anywhere near the stage it did. What I've realized, Claire, is that our family is way more important to me. As you are."

He let go of her hand and took her by the shoulders, turning her to face him. Against the white of his golfing shirt, his face and arms looked darkly tanned. His intelligent face was serious and sad.

"I love you, Claire. Is there any way I can make these past few months up to you?"

CHAPTER TWELVE

HE HADN'T SEEMED TO FEEL he loved her before he found out she was pregnant.

Claire pushed the negative thought aside. If she wanted to save this marriage, give her girls a happy, stable home, she was going to have to get past the bitterness and the hurt.

Under her breath, she repeated her new mantra: *An affair doesn't have to mean the end of a marriage.*

Kirk brought his hands up to caress the sides of her face. Cupping her jaw, he bent closer to her. "You *are* beautiful, Claire. As I watched you sleep this morning, it was all I could do not to climb in next to you."

So he *had* been the one to bring in the tray, to turn off the light.

"I'm fat." Was that all she could say? Claire could have bitten her tongue—wished she had.

Kirk's arms slipped around her waist, joining at the back, pulling her toward him. "You are not fat. You never have been."

"You can't deny that after Jenna—"

"Claire, I liked those full curves." He put a hand to her hair, stroking it. It was a calming gesture, and made her want to shut her eyes.

"Don't think this happened because of you—because of a few pounds or an extra wrinkle or two."

Janice was younger, and in truth that still stung. Forty was only a few years away, and Claire was all too aware of it.

"Because I love you. And I love your wrinkles. All two of them." Then he kissed her brow, his lips soft and comforting.

He loved her. How Claire wanted to believe that he meant what he said. His kisses—they felt as though he meant it. He was covering her face now, the tender skin of her eyelids, the sides of her cheeks, the line of her jaw.

She thought of last night, how her body had alternately glowed and ached with memories of the lovemaking they'd shared in the past.

It had seemed so impossible then, just twenty-four hours ago, that she would ever know those pleasures again.

Now she wasn't so sure.

"Kirk, I don't know..."

He was kissing the corners of her mouth, his lips still gentle and undemanding. "We have to start somewhere. I know it isn't going to be easy. But let me touch you, Claire. Let me show you how incredibly beautiful you are to me.''

His hands on her bare arms were so soothing, his kisses completely intoxicating. She didn't want him ever to move away from her. She felt a longing building from deep within, from the hurt, empty place at her very core.

Warmth flooded between her legs, and she pressed in against the muscled hardness of his thigh. His hands slid down from her shoulders, along the length of her back, pulling her closer, communicating his desire. Against her hipbone, she felt the hard bulge of his erection, and looked up to see him staring at the buttons on her blouse.

''You aren't wearing your bra.''

''I was sunbathing nude while you were away,'' she admitted. Although she had fair hair, her skin bronzed easily, just like Daisy's and Jenna's.

Kirk groaned. ''God, Claire. You drive me crazy sometimes. I wish I could have seen...''

He brought his hands up her sides, then trailed them just under the swell of her breasts. Lightly, he reached for the tiny white buttons on her blouse.

''So beautiful.'' Kirk took the weight of her breasts in his hands, drawing his thumbs over her nipples. Pleasure arced along her sensitized nerve endings.

''Ah.'' The soft sigh floated from her throat out into the night.

Kirk pulled her to the lounge chair where she'd lain only hours ago. As he undid the zipper of his shorts, he caught her gaze and asked, "Is this okay, Claire? I want to make love to you so badly...."

Was it okay? Was it even right?

Claire knew her thinking was foggy right now. He'd said he loved her, but did that erase all that he'd done?

And what about her? She wanted him right now—she couldn't deny that. But did she still love him? She didn't know the answer to that question.

"Claire?" Kirk eased her onto his lap, stroking her face, her hair. "Do you want to stop?"

His words were kind, his touch sweet, but sitting on top of him, she could feel how hard he was for her. And she was equally hot for him.

Maybe this was one of the ways for them to get closer, to repair the damage they both had suffered.

An affair doesn't have to mean the end of a marriage.

Claire placed her lips on his. Not a real kiss, just a touch. And whispered, her breath mingling with his, "Make love to me, Kirk. Right here. Right now."

IT WENT FINE; really, it did. Right up to the very last moment, when the shock waves had weakened to tremors, when Kirk had fallen to her side, their bodies still joined, their breathing still hard.

A sob choked out of Claire's throat, and she realized she wasn't fine. Not at all.

"What is it, Claire?" Kirk held her face to his shoulder.

She pulled back, unable to breathe. Pushing on his chest, she slid out from beside him and brushed back the hair from her face. Kirk was concerned, worried. He sat up and reached for her, but she moved quickly to the side, gathering her clothes, feeling the tears as they fell from her face onto her hands.

"You're scaring me, Claire. Please talk to me." But she just shook her head.

How could she have thought that all that was wrong between them could be solved so easily, so tidily? How could she have made love to this man, who had betrayed her, who at the very moment of coming inside her body had perhaps thought of someone else.

Janice.

She pulled on her shorts, her top, fumbled with buttons and the zipper. "You said you never made love to her. But did you kiss her? Did you touch her?"

Kirk's arms were wrapped around his bare chest. He looked confused, befuddled. "Let's not talk about that now, Claire. Please…"

"You did, didn't you? You kissed her…." God, this hurt, maybe more than anything else so far.

She wasn't surprised when he nodded, confirming her fears.

"Why do you want to ask these questions when the answers are only going to hurt you?"

"Because I need to know. You touched her, too, didn't you?"

She backed away, hating him then and hating *herself* even more.

Kirk stood but didn't try to approach this time. "No, I didn't touch her. Not in the way you mean."

So that was the bottom line, was it? He'd kissed Janice but had gone no further. *In real life.* But how about fantasy? If he'd been in love with Janice, he must have thought about her. Maybe even when he was making love with his wife. Maybe even this time...

Maybe thoughts of Janice, not Claire at all, had made him so hot...

She pushed through the screen, wanting only to put space between them. Oh, God, this hurt so much she couldn't stand it. She splashed water from the kitchen faucet over her face, but her shoulders were still heaving with her sobs.

She'd never cried like this in her life. Wrenching sobs that she simply could not control. He claimed he loved her, but how could he? No one would hurt someone he loved the way he had hurt her.

Kirk came inside, closing the screen carefully

behind him. "Please let me help you, Claire." His tone was anxious; she could see that he felt terrible, but it didn't matter. Nothing mattered except her need to cry.

A key chain hung on the hook by the door, and she grabbed it. She had to get out of this house before she woke the kids. "I'm going for a drive."

"Not like that." Kirk ran toward her. "You're in no condition—"

"Leave me alone!" She twisted from his arms and grabbed the door handle, her avenue for escape. "Leave me the hell alone!"

She realized she'd taken Kirk's car keys by mistake but didn't for a second consider going back inside to exchange them. Instead, she unlocked the front door of his sedan and slid behind the steering wheel. She could see Kirk standing at the kitchen window, looking gray faced and distressed.

She took comfort in the knowledge that he couldn't see her, sitting here in the dark. She'd thought to drive to some deserted laneway. Someplace safe and quiet, where she could be alone and just cry. But now she didn't want to move.

She didn't want to think, either, but unfortunately that was all she could do. Think of her husband and Janice, imagine them in each other's arms, mouths locked…

No! The picture was more than she could stand. Had he thought of her, Claire, at all? Had he felt any guilt at the moment he'd broken his wedding vows to her? Claire pressed the back of her hand against her mouth, wanting to erase the kisses she'd found so sweet earlier.

She glanced up. Kirk was still standing by the kitchen window. Did he have any idea how tempted she was to start the car and drive as far away from him as she could? She did not want to have to deal with this situation he'd placed them in. What woman would? To choose between living with a man who'd fallen in love with another woman or leaving him, thereby depriving her children of a safe, stable home with both their parents.

And she was pregnant! If she left Kirk, who would be with her in the delivery room when this child was born? When she gave that last push and the doctor announced the sex, was anyone going to care besides her?

Claire rested her arms and head on the steering wheel and allowed the sobs to explode from her chest. *No! No!* She cried until it hurt too much to cry anymore, and then she searched the car for a box of tissues.

She thought she'd put one in the glove compartment the last time she cleaned the car. She flicked the switch and the compartment door flew open, triggering a tiny interior light. Claire pushed past the car manual, the ice scraper, the map of Ontario.

No tissues. But something else was in there, something small, shiny, cool to the touch. She curled her fingers around it and pulled it out.

A tube of lipstick. And it wasn't hers.

Claire stuck the keys in the ignition and started the engine.

CHAPTER THIRTEEN

WHERE THE HELL was Claire going? She was too upset to be driving. Especially late at night on backcountry roads.

Kirk stepped away from the kitchen window and contemplated the remaining set of keys on the hook by the door. He was tempted to go after her, but he couldn't leave the kids alone.

Maybe where she was going at this time of night wasn't the point. She wasn't headed anywhere. She just couldn't stand to be in the same house with him anymore.

He'd never heard her cry like that before. To him the walls still echoed with the sound, bringing back another time, another place.

His mother and *his* father, arguing in the kitchen while he hid under the bed in his room. Shouted accusations, flung in both directions, followed by the slamming of the front door. And then sobbing.

Animal-pain sobs, the kind torn from your gut when mental pain becomes physical and your logical mind has simply given up.

That was what his dad had done to his mom, and that was what he'd done to Claire.

Kirk felt a sob of his own rising from his chest, and he quickly forced down a glass of water.

At least his kids hadn't witnessed the scene. At least they were safely asleep. He went into their rooms to check, then returned to the kitchen, where he reached into the cupboard over the fridge in search of brandy left over from last summer. There it was.

He pulled down the squat brown bottle and lined a tumbler with a couple of inches. Then he went out and sat on the slate steps, hoping the cooler night air might make it possible for him to draw a breath without feeling as if his lungs were about to cave from the weight of his guilt.

The brandy was gone in two minutes. He set the empty glass on the step and got up to pace the lane. He counted eighty-four steps to the top of the drive, which connected to the access road that led out to the highway. Which way had she turned once she got to the paved road? Toward Port Carling? Or Port Sandfield?

What did it matter? As if he could find her either way.

He retraced his steps to the cottage, the dark of the night pressing in on him, reminding him of his culpability.

And the real hell of it, the bitter irony, was that

only when he saw Claire break down had he realized how much he truly did love her. It was like that moment when he slipped on his glasses and all the stock quotes in the morning paper suddenly became legible.

He saw that his infatuation with Janice was precisely that. He saw that Claire was the woman he wanted to spend his life with. And he saw, God help him, how much he'd hurt her with his own confusion.

Sinking onto the top stair, he cupped his head in his hands and closed his eyes. *Please let her be all right. Please let her come back. Please let her give me another chance.*

Even if he didn't deserve it.

Old memories. At twenty-four, when he'd met her, Claire had been the kind of woman every young man dreamed about. Pretty, blond and buxom, with an outgoing personality and natural confidence to spare. He'd been amazed when she'd agreed to go out with him, and was soon captivated by her ability to see humor in almost every situation, and by her practical, no-nonsense intelligence.

His Claire.

He'd thought of her as such for years, even though he'd always sensed a core to her spirit where he was denied access. She was kind and caring to family and friends, with the strongest maternal instincts of any woman he'd known. But with him, she held something back.

Still, she'd been his friend, his lover, the mother of his children. Now he wondered why he hadn't been happy with that, why he had felt that she owed him something more. Something he himself couldn't really put words to.

KIRK WAS STILL ON THE STEP, his head cradled in his hands as he drifted in and out of sleep, but now he straightened his shoulders and looked ahead.

Although the sun hadn't yet risen, there was a lighter quality to the dark, or so it seemed to him. At a different pitch from the birds, which had already begun their morning chorus, he could clearly make out the sound of an approaching vehicle.

Soon, he saw the nose of his Volvo sedan through the screen of tree trunks. Claire, heading down the drive. Relieved, Kirk stood. It wasn't Claire, though. The car was his, all right, but Mallory was at the wheel. She parked about ten yards from him, then got out from the driver's seat reluctantly.

Mallory's brown curly hair was pulled back in a ponytail. She was wearing faded jeans with fraying hems, and a T-shirt short enough to reveal an inch of her flat belly. He noticed her feet were bare, and she carried something small in her left hand.

"Where's Claire?"

"She's at my place. Sleeping." Mallory pressed her lips together, then glanced at the bedroom windows of the cottage. "Are the girls okay?"

The question annoyed him. "Of course they're okay. They're sleeping. It's early in the morning. What in hell did you think they'd be doing?"

She took a step back. "Okay. Sorry. I didn't mean to accuse you of anything."

"Oh, really?" Then what was she doing here? She'd come to give him hell for hurting Claire. And he deserved it. He shoved his hands in his pockets and moved over toward the woodshed.

Mallory followed. "Claire is a mess, you know."

"I know." He pulled in a deep breath of air, then forced it out. He wished he could meet Mallory's gaze, but he was suddenly afraid he might break down. Staring at the ground, he choked out a few words. "Believe me, I feel terrible about that."

"I do believe you." Mallory put a hand on his shoulder.

He was surprised at the gesture. He'd expected Claire's friends to rally solidly behind her, against him. Certainly, Mallory and Drew had been cool enough toward him during lunch at the Conroys'.

"Drew and I want you guys to work this thing out," Mallory said. "And I still think you can. But you've got to appreciate how hard this is on Claire.

You know how she likes order in her life. This feeling of being out of control—well, it scares her. It certainly complicates matters that she's—"

"Pregnant." He picked up some stray logs the kids must have been playing with and threw them back on top of the stack he'd chopped last fall.

He turned to face Mallory. "I intend to look after her, to love her. If she'll let me..."

It worried him that now Mallory wouldn't look *him* in the eye. "I know, Kirk. But it might take some time. It doesn't help—" She sighed, then sat on the fat tree stump he used as a chopping block.

"What?" The block was big enough for two. He perched tentatively on the edge and looked down on Mallory's profile.

"She found this in the glove compartment of your car." Mallory opened her left hand, revealing a gold-colored tube of lipstick.

"Oh, hell."

Mallory passed it to him, and without thinking, he tossed it far into the trees and the scrub.

"It's Janice's, isn't it?"

"Yeah." Why the hell had she put the lipstick in his glove compartment? He remembered her pulling down the vanity mirror to freshen up the last time he'd taken her to dinner. That had been the night he'd revealed he was going to tell Claire about them. He groaned, thinking of the colossal mess he'd made of things.

"Seeing something tangible that belonged to Janice made the situation so much more real for Claire."

"Yeah. I can imagine how she would feel." How would he like it if he found another man's belongings in his wife's van? Just the idea made his chest swell with pain.

"Anyway—" Mallory stood and looked down at him "—Claire fell asleep just half an hour ago. I thought I'd let her sleep until she wakes up on her own. I'm not sure, but she'll probably come home then. She won't want to worry the kids."

"No," he agreed. To hell with him. She wouldn't care a bit for how he was feeling. And truthfully, could he blame her?

WHEN CLAIRE DROVE DOWN the lane toward the cottage shortly after nine in the morning, Andie was sitting on the front step, wearing cutoff jeans and an old soccer T-shirt. Her hair, which she obviously hadn't combed yet this morning, was a riot of red curls around her pale, freckled face.

The poor kid did not appear happy. Claire took a deep breath and glanced at herself in the side mirror as she got out of the car. She looked terrible—pale and red eyed—but hopefully Andie wouldn't notice.

"Good morning, hon. Have you had breakfast?"

"Daddy made pancakes." Andie stared down at her bare feet. "Where were you last night, Mom?"

Claire sat on the step next to her daughter. "Didn't Dad tell you?"

"He said you went to Mallory's. But why?"

The clear blue of her daughter's eyes was a potent truth serum. Claire drew a deep breath. "Your dad and I had an argument. And I needed—I needed—" Claire paused, shifting her gaze to the tall stand of trees by the woodshed.

"You know when you and your sister are fighting and I send you to your rooms to cool off?"

Andie nodded.

"Well, sometimes adults need to cool off, too."

"Is that what happened the last time you said Daddy went on a business trip? I saw his suitcase in the closet...."

Oh, my Lord. Claire remembered the way Kirk's clothing had been pushed to the side.

"He wasn't on a business trip, was he? You lied."

To protect you. Claire let her head sink onto her arms. "You're right, Andie. I should have told you the truth. But I didn't want you to worry." She trailed her fingers down Andie's soft cheek, then leaned in closer for a hug. Her daughter remained stiff, unyielding.

"I don't think it's very nice of you to go away when Daddy's only here for such a short time.

Maybe, if you were nicer to him, Daddy would want to come more often and stay longer.''

At times the demands of motherhood just were not fair. This was one of them. Was it her fault Kirk worked such long hours, had frequent business trips, often was tied up weekends? Didn't she wish he had more time for the family, too? But she would not say a word against Kirk to Andie.

''I'm sorry if you don't see as much of your dad as you'd like. But he's here today, right? Why not make the most of it.''

Andie considered that for a minute, before pushing herself into a standing position. ''Yeah. I guess.''

Guilt crushed Claire's ribs as she watched her daughter go back into the cottage. If she and Kirk were to get divorced, Andie would see even less of her father.

Yet Claire wasn't sure she could go back to living with Kirk as if nothing had ever happened.

Finding that lipstick in Kirk's glove compartment should have been such a little thing. After all, it didn't change a single thing she already knew about Janice and Kirk. Yet that slender metal tube had put an image in her head that she just could not shake.

Janice in the car next to Kirk. Gliding on her lipstick as she anticipated their dinner together.

And at the end of the evening…a kiss. That woman had kissed her husband.

And Kirk would have had to wipe all traces of that lipstick off before coming home to her, sliding between the sheets of their bed, mumbling some excuse or another.

Last night she'd seen the pain, the sorrow and regret, in Kirk's eyes. For the sake of her children, she wanted to forgive him. But in her heart, she just didn't know if it was possible.

CLAIRE WAS DETERMINED to keep busy that week while Kirk was back in the city. On Tuesday she had Mallory and Drew over for dinner. Then she invited Grady and the boys on Thursday.

She was amazed when both Warren and Taylor accepted the invitation. Between summer jobs, their reporting duties for the *Gazette* and wanting time with their friends, the twins had few spare hours. That night, however, they seemed relaxed and at ease. During dinner they teased the girls and each other, while managing to eat enormous quantities of the marinated flank steak that Claire had barbecued.

After dessert of ice cream and caramel-banana sauce, they good-naturedly agreed to take the girls out for a paddle on the lake. Claire and Grady helped with life jackets, then settled on the wooden chairs at the end of the pier to watch the chaos.

"Sometimes, they still act like such kids," Grady said, sounding a little nostalgic. He was leaning back in the chair, his long tanned legs planted firmly on the dock.

Claire watched as Warren maneuvered his paddleboat, which he was sharing with Andie, so that he could splash his brother in the face. "They look like they're having fun."

"Yeah. They're having a good summer. They went to their mom's last Sunday. She took them to a pool party at her boss's house and apparently he had a couple of really cute daughters. So that didn't hurt."

Claire smiled, enjoying the fine lines that sprang up around Grady's eyes when he grinned.

"Warren said she acted really proud when she introduced them to all her co-workers. You know, 'These are my boys,' that kind of thing. I think the boys appreciated being included in their mother's new life."

Claire nodded. She knew how overwhelmed they'd been when their stay-at-home mom had suddenly begun a new career and made new friends. That Bess's new life had included dumping her old husband hadn't helped. For a while the boys had felt that their mother had dumped them, as well, although the decision to have them stay in Port Carling so they could finish high school with all their friends had made sense.

"Lord, I can't believe this will be their last year of high school. I remember those days as if they were yesterday."

"Me, too." Claire looked down at her fingernails, which she'd painted pink that afternoon while the girls were playing outside, then glanced sideways at Grady. "That was the summer we went out for a few months. Do you ever think about those days?"

He seemed a little surprised by the question, but he nodded. "Sure do. I still can't believe I managed to date Claire Elizabeth Adams, class president and girl voted Most Popular..."

"Oh, stop it!" Her friends had teased her mercilessly about that Most Popular thing when she'd shown them her yearbook. "*You* were the guy all the girls wanted. Captain of the hockey team, most goals scored by any kid from Port Carling in one season...."

Grady hooted. "We were quite a team, weren't we?"

Was he talking about the hockey team or the two of them as a couple? Claire couldn't be sure, but she knew that she had never been as completely happy as in those few glorious months when she and Grady had dated.

Then Bess had told him she was pregnant.

"Do you ever wonder what might have happened...?"

"Sometimes." Grady cocked his head, his expression serious for once. "Yeah, sometimes I wonder...." His gaze brushed her face, the length of her body, like a caress. He reached out to touch her hand gently, then quickly withdrew.

Claire felt a sweet, piercing longing and closed her eyes so he wouldn't guess.

"But you and Kirk aren't going to end up like Bess and me," he said.

Claire wondered how he could sound so sure. Nevertheless, his statement put a full stop to her wayward thoughts. Now she took a deep breath, gathering her composure. "The divorce was awful, was it?"

"Oh, yeah. Bess and I had our differences, but I was definitely in the marriage for the long haul. Obviously, she wasn't."

He stared down at his hands. "Thankfully, I had to keep myself together for Warren and Taylor, or Lord knows what I might have done."

"And now you're seeing Terese...?"

Grady's face softened at the mention of her name. His lips curled up; the crinkles by his eyes returned. "She is one great lady, Claire, and her daughter sure is a funny little thing."

The kids had paddled out several hundred yards. Now they turned back. Claire was glad. A cool wind had picked up; the sun had dipped to tree level. She slipped on a sweatshirt and tried to work up a generosity of spirit toward Grady's new romance. "So things are going well?"

Grady's chest caved a little. "They were."

Were? Oh, she'd known there was something about that woman. "What's happened?"

"Terese's ex-husband managed to track her down this weekend. Lucky I was around or things could have gotten ugly for Terese and Lisa."

He flexed his hands, and Claire wondered if the situation had deteriorated to actual blows. "Mallory told me the reason she left the marriage in the first place was that he was physically abusive."

Grady nodded. "It started after Lisa was born. The occasional shove or slap. Once he gave Terese a shaking, then threw her against the stove. The corner of the metal handle caught her on the face—"

Claire closed her eyes briefly, sickened by the vivid mental picture she conjured. "Is that how she got that scar by her eye?"

"Yeah. But it wasn't enough to convince her to leave. She didn't reach that point until he turned on his own daughter. Then Terese knew she had no choice but to go."

"Thank God she did." Poor Terese and Lisa. Claire truly did feel sorry for them. But the idea of Grady having to deal with this man...

"You can say that again. Trouble is, having her ex show up has made her skittish. I took her into the police department. She filed a complaint, got a restraining order, but you only have to read a city newspaper to know how much protection that offers a woman.''

''Does she think he could be dangerous?''

''She does, and after seeing him in action, I don't blame her. The man is violent, Claire. And unpredictable. And now Terese wants to cool things off between the two of us because of him.''

''Really?'' Claire felt an uncomfortable twinge of guilt. Grady sounded so unhappy, but didn't she agree with Terese? She didn't want him in a situation where he'd have to worry about the constant threat of Terese's ex-husband.

''It's just like Terese to worry about me when she should be worrying about herself and her daughter. I want to protect her, but she won't let me!''

Maybe it's for the best. That was what she wanted to say, but Claire didn't dare. Grady wasn't the type to back away from a situation just because it might have dangerous repercussions for himself. He always thought of others first. But there was something she could remind him of.

''Just as long as the twins aren't dragged into this.''

Grady paused, looking out over the lake. Then he turned to her. ''I know what you're saying, Claire. Believe me, I'm worried, too. But Terese has done a lot for the boys, and they think the world of her. You know she's gone above and beyond in her role as high-school guidance counselor. Initially, her concern about the boys got us to spend time together.''

''Mallory told me.''

''The boys feel almost as protective about her as I do. And we all worry about Lisa.''

''Of course you do.'' The situation was hopeless. A man like Grady would never walk away from a woman who needed him, no matter what the potential danger to himself. Hadn't he gallantly stepped forward to marry Bess, even though he'd been in love with Claire at the time?

Claire wondered what it would feel like to be the woman in need and have Grady come to the rescue. She closed her eyes and let her head rest against the back of the chair. A cool breeze from the lake danced on her cheeks and lifted the wisps of hair around her face.

Grady to the rescue. It seemed to her that would feel mighty heady.

CHAPTER FOURTEEN

"WHAT I WORRY ABOUT," Claire said, shaving corn off the cob to make chowder for dinner, "is that this is Grady's transitional relationship. You know—to help him get over the divorce from Bess."

Mallory was standing by the stove, stirring the onions and green peppers she was sautéing on low heat. "You don't think he really loves Terese?"

"Oh, I don't know." Claire dismissed the question impatiently. "The point is, Grady was attracted to her, started seeing her, then this stuff with the ex-husband begins to simmer and now he's trapped. Don't you see?" She transferred the corn to the large pot where she'd been boiling diced potatoes in chicken stock, then added a cup of chopped ham. "A man like Grady is never going to back out on a damsel in distress."

"But why would he want to? Assuming he's in love with her."

"Maybe he just *thinks* he loves her. Because she needs him. Just the way Bess did when she found out she was pregnant."

"I see what you're getting at," Mallory said slowly. "But I also think you're wrong."

"Me wrong? Is that possible?" Claire joked, but inside she worried. Perhaps Mallory was too close to Terese to see the truth. Or was she herself out of line with her concerns about the new high-school guidance counselor?

Claire took the frying pan from Mallory and scraped the contents into the soup pot, then added a generous quantity of pepper to the mix. Tea biscuits were in the oven, and a tossed salad sat in the fridge. Dinner would be ready to eat in twenty minutes.

It was ladies' night at the Ridgeway cottage. Drew was in Toronto for a couple of days, recording an extra episode of *Foreign Matters* so that he and Mallory could take a few extra days over the long weekend. They were planning to drive to his cottage in the Gatineau Hills to do a little hiking and visit some of his old friends. Claire figured he was eager to show off his wife and daughter.

Since she wasn't expecting Kirk until later, Claire had invited Mallory and Angel for dinner. Right now the girls were playing outside on the swings.

"What time are you expecting Kirk?" Mallory asked as she laid napkins around the place settings.

"He doesn't usually get here until after eleven. With the long weekend traffic, though, it could be later.'' Claire couldn't believe it was the August long weekend already, the midsummer marker.

Last weekend she and Kirk had talked about taking the boat to Port Carling, something they hadn't done all summer. Driving there was faster, but traveling by boat was so much more romantic.

''How are things going?'' Mallory asked, her tone cautious.

''Well, the therapy sessions are kind of interesting.'' She'd read a book Riva Sharp had recommended, and she and Kirk had spent last Saturday night talking about the different issues it raised.

''And Kirk's been the model husband and father.'' Whenever he was here, he took over the bulk of the daily chores, insisting that she rest for several hours every afternoon.

Rest. If only she could. Sleep was so elusive these days.

She and Kirk handled each other with kid gloves. She could see he was eager not to hurt or upset her. There'd been no repeat of that intense lovemaking session they'd had on the deck.

In a way Claire was relieved. She was frightened of the emotions released in her only seconds after her soul-scorching climax. From ecstasy to agony. The phrase held more truth than she'd ever realized.

But she was almost as disappointed as she was relieved. Her body missed the physical contact.

Sometimes, she felt as if she were a teenager again the way her thoughts kept returning to sex. There was an aching in her breasts, an emptiness at her very core.

Did Kirk miss making love with her, too? Occasionally, she thought she saw a glimmer of awareness in his eyes when he was looking at her. A silence, a quickly gathered breath when she'd removed her cotton shirt to reveal a halter top that was a little small for this stage of her pregnancy.

But maybe she was imagining his reaction. Maybe it was only Janice he thought about, Janice he missed. She had to keep reminding herself that only after he'd discovered she was pregnant had he told her Janice was a mistake. His unborn child, not his wife, was his concern.

AT FIVE O'CLOCK they were about to sit down to their early dinner, when the phone rang.

Claire reached for the portable phone, which was sitting on the counter next to the sink. While she was in the kitchen, she grabbed the salad out of the fridge and passed it to Andie.

"Hello?"

"Hi, Claire, it's me."

"Kirk." Claire glanced down at the watch on her wrist. "When are you leaving?"

There was a pause. Claire's stomach muscles

tightened, and she noticed Andie watching her anxiously.

"That's why I'm calling. We've had some investors from New York show up. I'm expected to take them out for dinner tonight." He was using his business voice, all brisk, no nonsense. "I should be able to get away tomorrow around noon. There'll be less traffic then, anyway."

"Oh, yes, very sensible." Did he hear the sarcasm? If so, he pretended not to.

"Good. Tell the girls I love them. I'll be there in time for dinner, and we can take that boat trip to Port Carling on Sunday."

Claire swallowed, hating that she felt so disappointed. She kept telling herself she couldn't possibly love Kirk anymore, not after the way he'd betrayed her. But if that was true, why did she feel so bereft at having to wait an extra day to see him?

"Claire?" Kirk's voice was suddenly softer. "Are you there? Is everything okay?"

She turned her back to the table and went to the stove to check that the burner and the oven were shut off. They were. "I'm f-fine."

"Are you sure—"

Claire blinked back tears, and a flash of anger. How many times had she heard this same excuse from him in the past? How many times had family come second to work obligations? And how many times had those work obligations been a fabrication to give him time to spend with Janice?

"I have to go. We're just sitting down to dinner." She hung up the phone without waiting for his reply, then took her seat, half expecting the phone to ring again.

It didn't.

Claire avoided Mallory's eyes when she announced to her daughters that their father would be arriving later than expected. She played with the soup in her bowl and forced down a small serving of salad.

The baby. She had to eat for the baby's sake. Claire swallowed a mouthful of chowder, then another. For the first time in her life, she resented being pregnant. She didn't need this extra burden on top of everything else. Just once, she wished she could put her own wants and needs first.

And right now, she didn't want to eat. She wanted to rant and rave....

After the dishes were done, Mallory got the girls settled in front of the television with a movie in the VCR, then pulled her onto the deck to talk.

"Out with it, Claire. You look ready to explode."

"You don't know how right you are." Claire walked down the steps to the second level of the deck, and Mallory followed. From this vantage point, they could hear the rhythmic lapping of waves, the creaking of the boards at their feet. Claire gripped the railing and leaned against it.

"He says he has to entertain out-of-town clients. But I'll bet he's seeing *her*."

"Why do you think that?"

"Janice's holiday ended on Monday. I've been wondering how Kirk would react to seeing her back in the office."

"Did you try asking him?"

Claire bent to rest her forehead on her folded arms. How could Mallory understand? She and Drew were so close, so compatible. She couldn't appreciate what it was like to have your husband lie to you, deceive you.

"Claire, you can't worry yourself sick about things like this. You have to talk to Kirk. Tell him what you're thinking. Give him a chance to reassure you."

But what if he really was seeing Janice?

Well, at least she'd know.

"You're right," she decided. "I need to talk to Kirk. Will you stay overnight with the girls?"

"Now? You're going to talk to him now?"

"Just as soon as I can drive to Toronto. Let's see. It's five-thirty. If I leave right away I'll be there shortly before nine—I'll be going against the traffic."

"Oh, Claire. Are you sure this is a good idea? How will you know where to find him?"

"I'll call his assistant, Greer. She makes all his dinner reservations. So will you watch the girls?"

"Of course. But—"

"Talk to him," Claire reminded her, a finger at her friend's chest. "Your words. Remember?"

CLAIRE HAD CALLED Greer from her cell phone, shortly after heading the van south for Toronto.

"Good thing you caught me." Greer's voice had been cheerful. "I was just on my way out the door. His reservation is at that Italian restaurant he loves on Eglinton. Just a minute—I'll check my address book for the name—"

"No need. I know the one." She'd gone there with Kirk several times....

Now, parked in front of the restaurant, Claire considered the possibility that she wouldn't find them there. They might have chosen to spend their time somewhere more private. Would Kirk dare take Janice home? Claire's chest felt as if it were on fire as she imagined Janice tossing her purse on the chair by the front door, slipping her blazer onto the post by the staircase, walking up the steps, holding Kirk's hand...

No. No. He wouldn't stoop so low. Besides, it was only eight-forty. They had to still be here.

In the foyer she paused. There was a fountain in the center of the room, terra-cotta tiles on the floor, flamboyant Italian art on the walls. The place was crowded and noisy, and the enticing aromas of garlic, oregano and tomato sauce filled the air. A dark-haired girl in her early twenties—obviously the hostess—was standing nearby but preoccupied with a flirting customer. She laughed, tossing back shoulder-length hair.

The lights were dim, wrought-iron candelabra were on their lowest settings and candles on the tables flickered beckoningly.

The women were dressed to disarm. Reflexively, Claire put a hand to her hair, wishing she'd at least put on lipstick in the car. She was wearing a pale pink sundress and her old flat sandals, and couldn't have felt more out of place. Still, a man in his fifties smiled at her as their eyes caught across the room. And a nearby waiter bowed courteously.

"Meeting someone?"

"Yes. Could I just look around?"

He would have preferred to help, but she slid past, as elegantly as a woman who was four months pregnant could slide. She scanned the crowd, tables of lovers, of families, of friends, on the lookout for two furtive heads. One dark blond, the other brunette. Two people leaning in toward each other, possibly holding hands...

She would pour their wine over their heads, then throw Janice into the fountain. She would—

There was Kirk. She'd know those broad shoulders anywhere. A pillar hid the rest of the party from her view.

Claire moved forward. Now she saw the party in full. Two men were sitting with her husband. And he'd just noticed her.

In less than a second his eyes widened in astonishment, then narrowed with anger. She knew that set to his mouth, even though she saw it rarely.

Suddenly, she felt absurd, conspicuous. He wasn't with Janice; her suspicions had been unfounded. What on earth was she going to do now? Turn and drive back to the cottage?

Kirk had risen, and his companions were looking her way. Somehow Claire propelled herself forward. Kirk was smiling now, all genial charm.

"You made it, Claire. Better late than never. This is my wife, gentlemen. I asked her to join us if she could."

His hand on her arm was gentle as he guided her to the chair on his right. The two men across the table did not seem upset by the interruption. Both slightly older than Kirk, both dressed in similar business attire as her husband, they smiled politely and held out their hands in turn.

"Claire, Martin McIntyre and Barry Stracker. They've come from New York to consider investment opportunities in some of our newer high-tech ventures."

Claire smiled at Barry, who sat across from her.

He had a round face, balancing keen eyes with a warm smile. Martin, sitting across from Kirk, was both taller and better looking, and his expression was decidedly more aloof.

"I hope I'm not interrupting anything important," she said. "When Kirk told me about the dinner, I thought I couldn't come, but at the last minute I found a sitter."

"I'm glad." Kirk smiled at her, and for a moment she almost believed that he was pleased to see her. Then she remembered whom they were with, and the need to present a pleasant facade.

"We were just about to order our main course," Barry said. "Would you like to see the menu?"

He handed her the leather-bound booklet, and she smiled her thanks. Eating was the last thing on her mind, but of course she'd have to order now that she was here.

"The server told us about a pasta special you'd probably like," Kirk said. "A mixture of ricotta and spinach in homemade ravioli, served with a creamy tomato sauce."

"That does sound good."

The server had just returned and was gathering menus. Claire added hers to the pile.

"And a salad on the side?" Kirk asked. "Claire's pregnant," he announced to the group, putting an arm around her shoulders.

"Congratulations!" Wineglasses were raised, then the orders were given.

Claire asked for a nonalcoholic cocktail, then sat back in her chair. The suspicion and anger that had fueled her during the long drive had completely fizzled, and now she felt an odd mixture of contentment and pleasure. Kirk hadn't removed his arm, and its warmth felt inclusive, as if he were shepherding her into the group, assuring her of her welcome.

Barry was charming and gregarious, and she soon found that Martin had a dry wit, which he used sparingly but effectively.

"Your husband is a persuasive man," Barry said, breaking a piece of bread in his hands. "But what does his wife say? Should we hand him the six hundred thousand dollars he's asking for?"

"Only if you can't afford seven," Claire said.

Kirk laughed and squeezed her shoulder. "As you can see, we make quite a team."

Briefly, Claire allowed her gaze to meet his, and was surprised at the warmth and affection she saw. Balling her napkin in one fist, she willed herself to hold back quick tears.

"And do you already have children?" Barry asked, jumping topics with ease.

"Three girls," Kirk said proudly.

"Maybe a son this time?" Barry glanced at Claire, then back to Kirk.

"Or perhaps they'll stick to the house specialty," Martin said. "My wife says once you get the recipe figured out, don't bother experimenting. We have two boys."

Their meals arrived then, and Claire was surprised to find she felt famished. The ravioli were so tender they melted like shortbread in her mouth, and the seasonings were exquisite. The salad was tossed with a light raspberry vinaigrette and served with a handful of berries and some freshly roasted pecans in the center.

"Oh, my Lord," Claire said after her first few bites. "No wonder you like this restaurant so much."

"It is good, isn't it?" Kirk said. He'd ordered a pistachio chicken dish, served with oven-roasted vegetables.

"Just give me ten minutes with that chef..." She was thinking of gathering new recipes for her cooking column, but Martin chose to misinterpret her intent.

"I'm not so sure that would be wise." He glanced up from his osso buco Milanese. "The man was quite handsome—I saw him as I passed by the kitchen on the way to the washrooms. Thin as a rake, with dark Italian eyes. Pregnant or not, I wouldn't trust my wife alone with him. Besides, aren't those Italians partial to blondes?"

Kirk returned his arm to her shoulders. "I won't let her go alone, then."

The banter was flattering, even though she knew she wasn't looking her best. Then she caught a glimpse of herself in a mirror on the opposite wall, and was amazed to see she looked okay. Her hair fell in pale yellow waves around her face, and the warm atmosphere and camaraderie at the table had brought color to her cheeks and lips.

The meal ended too quickly. Kirk picked up the tab for the group, then the four of them rose from the table and walked single file to the front door, with Claire leading the way.

She paused in the foyer, suddenly guilty about having interrupted. "But did you get to discuss all your business issues?"

"Madam—" Barry took her hand and bowed slightly "—meeting an associate's wife is as important as reviewing the financial statements."

"Often more so," Martin said dryly.

"We discussed the project over drinks before dinner," Kirk assured her. "These gentlemen have to get back to their hotel. They have an early flight home tomorrow morning. If you have questions," he said, turning to them and shaking hands, "you have my cell phone number, as well as the number at work."

Out on the street he hailed them a cab, and Claire smiled as they made their final goodbyes.

"You must come to New York and we'll return the hospitality," Barry said.

"Yes," Martin added over his shoulder. "The food might not taste any better, but it'll be twice as expensive."

The cab door shut and they were off. Claire was still smiling as she watched the red taillights disappear down the street. She was about to tell Kirk how much she'd enjoyed the evening, when she noticed he was staring at her. And the angry expression she'd glimpsed at the restaurant had returned.

"What are you doing here, Claire?" he asked. "You were checking up on me, weren't you?"

CHAPTER FIFTEEN

"AND IF I WAS CHECKING UP on you?" Claire squared off against her husband. "Would you blame me?"

All the goodwill she'd been feeling vanished into the warm, humid night air. She forgot about the pleasure of the past hour and a half and remembered, instead, the anger that had fueled her trip in the first place.

"Janice was back in the office this week, wasn't she?"

"So what if she was?" Kirk's hands were in his trouser pockets. He took a step closer, lowered his voice a notch.

"Claire, I'm going to counseling with you. I'm spending every spare moment I have with you and the kids. If that isn't enough to convince you I'm serious about making this marriage work, then maybe you should tell me what it is that you want?"

Claire gathered her courage to ask the burning question, afraid of the answer but unable to live any longer with the uncertainty. "I want to know what your feelings are for Janice. Do you still love her?''

Kirk's shoulders heaved on a sigh, then he shook his head in a gesture of hopelessness. ''Oh, Claire.''

She stepped back, knowing the question had been a mistake. ''I'm going ho—''

''No. You're not leaving.'' Suddenly, Kirk was in front of her, his hand on her arm. ''We need to talk, but not here. Come back to the house, Claire.''

She jerked away from him. ''Don't tell me what to do.''

He covered the side of his face with his hand, shooting a glance heavenward, then at her again. ''I'm sorry, Claire. I just couldn't stand it if you left now. Please, let's have a calm, civilized talk.''

Claire considered. He was right on one point. They couldn't remain here on the street, arguing about something this important. ''I suppose.''

Kirk walked her to the van and held the door as she climbed inside.

''My car's just down the block. I'll meet you at home.''

Home. What was home anymore? Claire felt oddly disoriented as she drove the familiar streets. The freeway took her quickly to their neighborhood in Richmond Hill. Here the houses were large, most of them brick, with generous lots and mature trees and landscaping.

She pulled into her driveway, noting that Kirk had been keeping the lawn in good condition. The garage door was already open; Kirk's Volvo nosed into the right-hand side as usual.

Just as she got out of the van, Kirk opened the door that led from the garage to the house. "Come in, Claire."

"Thanks for the invitation. Last I checked, I owned this place, too."

Kirk's jaw tightened. "I'm going to ignore that."

For a second, Claire was ashamed of her little temper, but then she decided she was entitled to feel angry. Maybe not about his opening the door but about other, more important, things.

She swept through the hallway and into the kitchen, aware that everything was neat and clean—not so much as a dirty glass by the sink. In the family room she paced the length of the fireplace. The house was so quiet she could hear the hum of the air-conditioning.

"Want a drink?"

"No, I don't want a drink."

She watched Kirk lower himself onto their well-worn leather sofa. After a few uncomfortable moments she propped herself against the arm at the opposite side, and he twisted to face her.

"When you asked if I was over Janice, I didn't mean to avoid the question."

"Really?" Claire picked at the polish on one fingernail, wondering if she was ready to hear this. He was taking so long to reply the news had to be bad. Maybe he didn't know how to tell her. After a long silence, she couldn't bear it anymore. "You aren't over her, are you?"

"No, I'm not," he agreed.

Pain knifed a line from her throat to her gut. Her mouth opened automatically for air, just as she realized he was still speaking.

"Because there was nothing to get over. Not really. It was just an infatuation. I see it quite clearly now. I never loved her at all. Not the way I love you. The way I've loved you our entire twelve years together."

He took her hands and clasped them, and he looked so sincere she was tempted to believe him. The fight went out of her then, and she realized that what she'd really felt all along was fear.

"Are you sure, Kirk? Or are you just saying so because of the baby?"

He glanced at her waist. The small mound that was their child was barely visible behind her full dress. He tugged on her hands until she was leaning close enough that he could wrap one arm around her neck.

"The baby matters. Just as all three of our other

children matter. But that doesn't change the fact that I love you."

Was she a fool to believe him? But she did. Or maybe she just *wanted* to. With a whimper she let him draw her near, until her face was securely on his shoulder, her body tucked in next to his. She felt him trace the outline of her mouth with a finger and allowed her lips to part slightly, her tongue to flick against his skin ever so briefly.

"Oh, Claire." He bent his mouth to hers, his lips firm and warm. For several seconds she and he were still, then her mouth parted wider and his lips became more demanding. Stroking, brushing, nibbling.

"Claire," he said again, pulling back for a moment. "When I kiss you, I kiss only you. Always."

She knew what he was telling her, and couldn't stop a tear from slipping out the corner of her eye. She saw his concern when he tasted its saltiness and edged away to read her expression.

"Happy this time," she said, running her hand along the corded muscle that stretched across the breadth of his shoulder.

"Are you sure?" He kissed her eyelids gently, while his hands teased the strands of her hair. "I want to make love to you, Claire. But if you cry again, God help me, I think I'll want to die."

No longer angry, or even jealous, Claire traced the outline of her husband's strong face, stopping briefly at the velvet softness of his earlobe, then continuing along the curve of his ear to the tangle of curls falling over his broad forehead.

"I can't promise not to cry," she said. "But this time I won't run away."

RECORDED JAZZ MUSIC, played by her favorite saxophonist, awoke Claire the next morning, the music like a long, lazy caress. She opened her eyes in time to see Kirk walk in the door with a tray.

He wore only his white cotton boxers, and she admired the sculpted muscles of his chest, the tapering of his hips, the long line of his legs.

"Bagels and juice?" He set the tray on the bed, then scrambled under the covers with her. He'd turned off the air-conditioning and opened the windows to sunshine and the faintest of breezes.

"You're spoiling me." She stretched with a purr, then leaned back against the headboard. "Although truth is, I *am* starving."

"Must be that small dinner you had last night," he teased, spreading strawberry jam over cream cheese. "Want this?"

"Mmm." The bagel was still warm, toasted to just the right crispness, and the tang of the cream cheese beautifully offset the sweetness of the jam.

She hadn't realized she'd closed her eyes until she opened them and saw Kirk observing her.

"Watching you eat is always such a pleasure. You turn food into a sensual experience."

"Isn't it for everyone?" She offered him some bagel and he took a bite. "Come on. Tell me that isn't the second best thing to sex."

"What about chocolate?" he asked, nibbling the fingers holding the bagel. "Researchers say some women prefer chocolate to sex."

"A close second," she admitted, catching her breath as his nibbling turned to kisses traveling the length of her arm. She set the bagel on the tray and shut her eyes. "Mmm, yes. That feels nice."

He stopped at her shoulder and eased down the spaghetti strap of her nightgown to expose a full breast. Cupping it with one hand, he lowered his mouth to the butterscotch-colored nipple and, after a gentle, teasing tug, looked back at her. "Better than chocolate?"

"If only there were a way to combine the two."

"I can think of a few..."

"I'll bet you can." She chuckled, then sank lower into the pillows. "But then sex would become fattening. Something I definitely don't need."

Kirk was at her tummy now, nuzzling his face against her skin. He rested one cheek on her for a moment, and his expression grew serious. "You're always talking as if you have some sort of weight problem, but you know that you don't, right?"

Claire squirmed. "I know I'm not supposed to do anything crazy like try to lose weight when I'm pregnant."

"Pregnant or not, you're perfect as you are. Did you notice the men watching you in the restaurant last night? Not just the guys at our table but several others, as well. You're incredibly pretty. I felt so lucky it was me you were with."

Claire remembered the protective arm over her shoulders and smiled a little. No way was she as gorgeous as he was making her sound. She'd been in a sundress and flat sandals, after all. But she felt he meant what he was saying. And maybe she was that pretty. To him.

They made love between bites of bagel and swallows of juice. It turned into a game. Just when Claire thought desire was going to sweep them over the edge, Kirk would make them stop and take another mouthful.

"But I don't want to eat!" she protested against his shoulder, her body coiled tightly with desire.

"Be patient."

So she bit and chewed and swallowed. And was rewarded as Kirk's hard, sleek body rose up above her, then entered smoothly. By this point they were so turned on there was no stopping either of them.

Ten minutes later, they were breathless in each other's arms, sated in every possible sense of the word. The breakfast tray was empty, the CD had finished playing and their lovemaking was most satisfyingly concluded.

"I love you, Claire."

Kirk squeezed her tight, and she closed her eyes on tears of pleasure.

"This has been the most wonderful morning of my life."

"I'm glad. Me, too." He kissed her softly, then stretched out his legs. "How long is Mallory able to watch the kids?"

"The kids!" Claire sat up straight, unable to believe she'd all but forgotten about them. "Poor Mallory. I never did tell her what time I'd be back."

"Relax," Kirk said, but he sat up, also. "We can call her on the cell phone on the drive up. Let's grab a quick shower so we can hit the road."

"Okay." Claire swung her legs over the side of the bed, then stood, naked. Her nightgown was somewhere in the pile of bedding tangled on the floor. Aware of Kirk's gaze, she automatically lifted her hands to her belly, then she forced them down. If he thought she was so perfect the way she was, then let him see.

She was rewarded by his grin. "Beautiful," he confirmed.

She smiled all the way to the bathroom. Quickly, she brushed her teeth. As soon as she shut off the faucet she caught the sound of Kirk's voice from around the corner.

He was talking to someone.

Claire's heart jumped. The happy hours they'd spent in bed were forgotten as it occurred to her that he could have planned to meet Janice after his business meeting. Maybe he was calling her now to apologize for not showing up earlier.

Walking quietly, she padded around the corner and found him with his back to her.

"I'm sorry," he was saying to the person on the other end of the line.

Claire's hand went to her throat. Wide-eyed, she watched him turn toward her. The relaxed expression on his face suddenly tightened. His smoky eyes narrowed, and his chest heaved with an indrawn breath.

"It's Mallory," he said. Holding out the receiver to Claire, he asked, "Do you want to speak with her?"

The panicked feeling whooshed out of her, leaving her ashamed and vulnerable. She reached for a robe she kept on the back of the door and shook her head.

"I insist," Kirk said between clenched teeth. "Or how else will you know I'm telling the truth?"

She shook her head. "I know. I'm sorry—"

"Take it." He dropped the receiver on the bed and left the room.

Claire wrapped the robe tightly over her breasts, glanced at the receiver, then down the hall. Kirk had disappeared into the girls' bathroom. A moment later she heard the shower.

Tentatively, she reached for the phone. "Mallory?"

"What's going on there? One minute I'm talking to Kirk, the next—silence."

"I guess the poison I put in his morning coffee had a sudden effect."

"Claire…"

"Of course I'm joking. He's in the shower. Alive and well, I promise." But not happy. Definitely not happy. "We'll be leaving shortly. Were the girls okay?"

"Yeah, although Andie had a hard time falling asleep."

Claire thought of her eldest daughter and sighed. "I'm sorry about that, but thanks for holding down the fort."

"It was fun. We made French toast for breakfast. Daisy showed me how. We're about to go to the Conroys' beach."

"We'll meet you there."

Claire was dressed and waiting by the time Kirk came downstairs. She'd made their bed and done the breakfast dishes. Now she was watering the indoor plants, which didn't seem to need it. Kirk had taken good care of those, too.

"Ready?" Kirk asked her. His tone was brisk, his expression remote.

Claire knew she'd hurt him with her suspicions. But could he really blame her? If the situation were reversed, would he be so quick to forgive and forget?

CHAPTER SIXTEEN

"ANDREA? PLEASE TELL ME what's bothering you." Claire rested her arms on the mattress of the top bunk. Andie was lying with her face to the wall. She'd sat stone-faced in the car on the drive home from the Conroys' beach and rushed straight to her room the second the car stopped.

"Please, honey. I can see how unhappy you are and I want to help."

Andie's shoulders started to shake. "Go away."

"Oh, honey." Claire looked uncertainly at the small wooden ladder, then shrugged. "If you're not coming down, then I'll have to come up. I only hope this old bed can take the weight."

Claire gathered her skirt around her legs and climbed. Once up, she stretched out beside her daughter and tentatively ran a hand down her arm.

"Honey, I know you were disappointed your daddy was late, but we're still going to make the boat trip to Port Carling. First thing in the morning."

"I don't want to go."

Andie was pouting, being childish; it reminded

Claire of the battles they'd had when her daughter was three.

"Andie, you know you love going to Port Carling by boat."

"It'll be boring."

"Boring?" Claire tried to put herself in the ten-year-old's head. "You miss your friends, right? I told you we should have invited—"

"Oh, Mom-m-m-m." Andie rolled onto her tummy and planted her face in her pillow.

It was a cue to leave, Claire supposed. But this time she wasn't going to. She was just too worried. Andie didn't want to talk, but maybe it was time to force the issue.

"This has something to do with your friend Erin, doesn't it?"

"Erin?"

"You two were so close at the beginning of the year. Until Christmas. What happened, Andie? Did Erin do something that upset you?"

Now Andie rolled over on her back. Her eyes gleamed with leftover tears as she stared up at the ceiling. "No, Mom. I just got bored with her, okay?"

Claire examined her daughter's face. This was definitely not ringing true. "I thought she was always friendly and fun to be around. And her parents seemed like such a nice couple."

"They're getting a divorce."

"They are?"

Claire remembered the last occasion she'd seen Erin's parents. It was just after her interview with Andie's teacher in March. They'd discussed Andie's poor results on the second-term report card, and Claire had been a little teary eyed when she'd spotted the attractive pair waiting for their turn. They'd been very polite and calm; asked after Andie and said they missed seeing her around. Claire never would have guessed they were having any problems.

"Now Erin spends half her time with her mom and half her time with her dad."

"Oh." Claire reflected for a minute. "And when did this happen? Her parents separating, I mean."

"Day after Christmas." Andie blinked, still staring up at the ceiling.

After Christmas. Which was when Andie's marks had begun to dive. Claire propped her head up on her elbow. "Honey, just because her parents are no longer together doesn't mean you can't be friends. In fact, Erin probably needs—"

"Forget it, Mom, okay? Just forget it! You don't understand anything!" Andie twisted her body up from the mattress and crawled over Claire's legs to get to the ladder. Claire tried to rush after her, but the folds of her long skirt snared her.

"Wait, Andie!"

Slam! The door was shut, her daughter gone. A moment later Claire heard the screen door slam, too.

CLAIRE TALKED the situation over with Kirk that night. "I just don't know what to do."

"Maybe we should speak to Erin's parents in September. See if they have an idea what happened between the girls."

"That's a good idea." But September was a month away, and Claire wished she could help Andie *now*.

"Let's hope the boat trip tomorrow snaps her out of her funk."

It did, but not at the beginning. Andie was the last one to the boat the next morning, and when she did finally show up, she'd forgotten her hat and they all had to wait while she ran back to the cottage for it.

"Hurry up, Andie," Daisy complained.

"Oh, just shut up," Andie snapped.

"Andie," Kirk warned. He shot a concerned glance at Claire before starting the motor of their mahogany launch. Carefully, he backed the old boat—which Grady had lovingly restored to its original condition a few years ago—out of the boathouse. Soon they were cruising and Claire had wind in her face and ears and the smell of lake water and gasoline fumes in her nose.

She squinted out across the water, which shimmered in the high sun. The shoreline was dotted with cottages. Some were enormous, sprawling buildings, others medium-size like theirs, and a few were small and rustic. While she appreciated the conveniences of her place, the smaller ones were her favorite. They snuggled into the land better; sometimes you could see only the windows, peering like eyes from amid the weathered old trees.

No matter which direction you looked there were other boats. A couple were pulling skiers. Claire noticed Kirk steer carefully away from them.

Conversation was difficult because of the noise from the motor and the breeze whipped up by the boat, but she thought she sensed everyone in the family relaxing. She passed out soft drinks, then leaned back into her seat, determined to enjoy the day.

Even with the breeze it was warm, and Claire was glad for her icy soda. She sucked through the small tab opening and tilted her head a little in Kirk's direction.

He was sitting on the back of his chair, one hand on the steering wheel, the other cupping the cola she'd given him. The wind had flattened the curls at the top of his head, and the sides of his short-sleeved shirt, which he wore unbuttoned, sounded like flags as they flapped in the breeze. Despite spending only weekends at the cottage, he was as tanned as Claire.

Kirk slowed his speed as they neared Port Carling and joined the queue of watercraft waiting to tie up at the wooden piers.

"Can we visit Mallory and Angel?" Daisy asked. The lenses on her sunglasses were shaped like flowers, and just looking at her middle daughter made Claire smile. Of all three children, Daisy was the most fashion conscious. Today she had on a matching short set with a swing top of pale yellow, yet another flower gracing the front.

"Sorry, Day. The Driscolls are away, remember?" Kirk had stilled the motor. Now he grabbed for the dock. Once he got a grip he pulled the boat up close so they could disembark.

Claire tied the boat to one of the metal rings screwed onto the pier, before reaching over to give Jenna a hand.

"Who's going to print the *Hub of the Lakes Gazette?*" Andie asked.

"I think the staff are taking over for this edition. Drew wrote his editorial ahead of time."

"Can we go to the fudgery, then?" Daisy asked.

"I want an ice cream." Jenna crossed her arms, indicating she would not negotiate.

Even Andie had her request. "Can we look at the bookstore?"

"We'll do everything," Kirk promised, taking

Jenna's hand in his. Claire was surprised when he took hers, too.

They'd barely touched since arriving at the cottage yesterday afternoon. Barely talked.

Now he squeezed her hand as all five of them moved along the dock. They crossed over the bridge and came to the bookstore.

"We'll stop on the way back," Kirk promised, ushering them past the community center, toward Steamboat Bay.

"Ice cream?" Kirk asked as they approached the take-out window at Nibbs.

The girls ran ahead, and Claire smiled. "Finally, an indulgence a pregnant woman can really appreciate."

Kirk raised one eyebrow. "I can think of others." He tugged her closer. "Remember?"

Oh, she remembered all right. She was surprised to hear him speak of it, though. They'd been so careful of each other, so polite since that dreadful misunderstanding about the phone call. Of course, they'd had little time with the girls around.

"What flavor, Claire?" Kirk asked, after the girls had been served and were settled on an outdoor bench.

Claire looked through the glass display at the many tempting tubs of exotic flavors and old favorites. "Cookies and cream. No, maple pecan. Oh, I can't decide."

"A scoop of each," Kirk told the lady behind the counter. "One for you, one for the baby," he said, passing her the cone. He'd chosen black licorice, a flavor Claire just did not get.

"Oh, Daddy," Jenna said the moment she saw it. "That looks gross."

"Want a taste?" Kirk put the cone inches from her lips.

"Ick!" Jenna turned her head. So did Andie and Daisy when he tried to get them to sample it.

"Now you know why I order this flavor," he said, enjoying a big bite from the scoop. "I don't have to share."

The rest of them took nibbles from one another's cones. Claire sampled Jenna's bubblegum, Daisy's chocolate mint and Andie's double chocolate.

Jenna finished her cone first, then tried to slide onto her mother's lap to have some of hers. After she slid off a second time, she put her hands on her hips and complained, "Why is your lap getting so fat, Mommy? I can't fit there anymore."

Claire glanced over at Kirk and saw that he was equally surprised and amused by the comment. So far they hadn't mentioned the new baby to the children. Was this the time? He nodded slightly.

"Because I'm going to have another baby."

"You are?" Andie froze, then looked from her mother to her father. "When?"

"Around the middle of January, I think," Claire said.

"Will it be a boy or girl?" Daisy asked.

"We don't know."

"Can we hang a stocking at Christmas for the baby?" Jenna wondered.

"You bet."

"Will I get to help take care of it?" Andie asked. "I'll be eleven by then."

"I'm sure you'll be a big help," Kirk said, stroking down one of her wild red curls. Claire wondered, would this baby be another redhead? Or a blonde like the others?

"Me, too?" Daisy asked.

"There'll be work enough for all of us, I'm sure." Claire felt exhausted just remembering what those first few months were like. Night feedings weren't too bad with only one child to care for, but she had three children already, and a household to run. And maybe she'd be on her own besides.

Suddenly, her ice cream didn't taste that great. She surreptitiously dumped it in the trash, then followed her family across the parking lot to the first of the appealing shops in Steamboat Bay.

As she was fingering children's sweatshirts marked down twenty percent, Kirk came up beside her.

"Funny, but when we were telling the girls

about the new baby, I realized that I didn't even know how you felt about having a fourth child.''

That was true. They hadn't talked about it. ''I guess we've had a lot on our mind.''

''But still—'' Kirk tucked a hand under her elbow. ''You look so tired. I was wondering if we should consider hiring some extra help. For the first few months, anyway.''

Claire just shook her head and walked out of the store. She knew Kirk was trying to be considerate, but she didn't want a stranger inside her house. She wanted a husband she could count on every now and then.

''Daddy!'' Jenna pointed to a window display. ''Beanie Babies! Can I go inside to see them?''

''Sure,'' Kirk said from behind her. ''Take your sisters with you and we'll wait out here.''

Kirk popped the last of his cone in his mouth. ''That was good.''

''Really?'' Claire couldn't believe it. ''It looked like you were eating tar.''

''Tar.'' Kirk pretended to consider the new title. ''Sounds interesting. Maybe you could put the recipe in your 'Cottage Cooking' column.''

She punched his arm lightly. ''Don't make fun of my column.''

His lower lip rounded. ''Sensitive, are we?''

Claire ducked her head. That she loved her column as much as she did seemed silly, but she felt enormous satisfaction when she saw her few short paragraphs and the accompanying recipes printed each week, along with the tiny photograph that Drew had taken of her last Thanksgiving.

She hadn't told anyone, but she could imagine printing a cookbook in a few years. *The Cottage Cooking Collection.* She'd always wanted to write a cookbook; this could be the perfect opportunity.

Kirk lifted the side of her sunglasses and inspected her. "Now what are you thinking about?"

He always bugged her for not sharing her thoughts. But this cookbook idea was still so new. "Nothing."

"Oh?"

His hand on hers loosened slightly, and she wondered if she'd imagined the icicles hanging off that one word. She tightened her grip and was about to ask him what the problem was, when she saw he was watching someone else.

Glancing ahead, she saw Terese and her daughter, Lisa. A moment later her girls had spotted Lisa, and soon the four of them were chattering.

"Hi, Terese." Kirk stepped forward, smiling.

He'd met Terese a few times now, although Claire couldn't remember if she'd told him Terese and Grady were dating.

"Hello, Kirk, Claire." Terese's usually friendly smile looked a little flat today.

"Enjoying the summer?" Claire asked, trying

not to focus on Terese's tightly cinched belt. Her waist couldn't be twenty inches. On a grown woman, that was practically obscene. She thought, with regret, of the double-scooped ice-cream cone she'd all but finished.

"It's so nice to spend the time with Lisa," Terese said. "And I'm doing a little painting."

"Will you have a showing?" Kirk asked.

"Oh, nothing as fancy as that," Terese said modestly. "Mallory's offered to put up a few of my canvases in her store to see if there's any interest. In fact, she has one in her window now."

"That was yours?" Kirk glanced at Claire.

As they'd passed the store they'd admired the stark contrast of granite rock and rippling water. Claire had felt the two elements were somehow at war in the picture.

"You're very talented," she said, meaning it.

"Thanks. I've always wanted the chance to paint in lake country."

Unable to stop herself, Claire asked, "What's Grady up to today?"

Terese lowered her gaze. One black-sandaled foot stepped back. "Actually, we haven't seen much of each other lately. I've been busy with Lisa and painting, and Grady's working on a special custom order."

The news should have come as a relief, but how could anyone be glad at Terese's obvious unhappiness? Her averted eyes were heavy with sorrow, and something else. Resignation?

"The girls sure seem to get along," Kirk said, turning back to watch the four of them climb all over the bench where they'd sat with their ice creams earlier.

"Lisa loves your daughters," Terese said, her lips curling upward briefly.

"Why don't you bring her over for lunch tomorrow." Kirk looked at Claire. "We have no other plans, do we?"

"None. That's a great idea," Claire said, as if the impromptu invitation were not at all unusual. In truth, Kirk was rarely the one to instigate social gatherings; he usually left the entertaining schedule up to her. Maybe he was just trying to avoid spending time alone with her before he had to leave to go back to Toronto.

Once they'd settled on when and Claire had agreed to allow Terese to bring ice-cream treats for the girls but not dessert for the adults, Terese and Lisa continued with their errands and Kirk tucked Claire's hand under his arm.

"She looks unhappy. Do you think she's lonely?"

They stopped outside a store window, watching as their girls went inside to admire another display of small stuffed animals.

"Quite possibly." Claire outlined the facts of

Terese's romance with Grady, then the upsetting visit from her ex-husband.

"Poor woman. What a burden. Is she taking legal action against him?"

"I know Grady drove her over to the police and they got a court order for him to stay away."

"She's so tiny..." Kirk shook his head. "That scar above her eye...?"

Claire nodded. "Apparently, he threw her against the stove one night."

"And this romance thing with Grady—is it off, then?"

Claire thought back to Terese's unhappy face, to Grady's recent admission that things were at an impasse between them. "I'm not sure."

"It's not like Grady to back away from a woman who needs help."

Wasn't that the truth? "Maybe he can help her more if he's not romantically involved...."

Kirk pulled back and scrutinized her. "Perhaps we should invite him to lunch, as well."

"Really, Kirk. Playing matchmaker isn't your style."

"Could be I have my reasons."

Claire considered it an odd thing for him to say, but she didn't get a chance to pursue the matter because he immediately changed the subject.

CHAPTER SEVENTEEN

THE NEXT MORNING Claire woke up before anyone else—or so she thought until she went out into the living area and found the couch empty, Kirk's blankets neatly folded on a trunk they kept on the window wall. Sliding open the patio door, she pulled her thin robe to her chest, then walked to the railing and leaned over.

Kirk stood poised at the edge of the lower deck, hands raised above his head in a vee. He was wearing his swimming trunks. Claire had a second to admire his well-toned body. He pushed off, and his body pierced the surface of the lake with hardly a splash. For a long moment he remained submerged.

When he finally came up for air Claire realized she'd held her breath from the moment he'd gone under.

She watched as he struck out, swimming parallel to the shore, until he was out of sight around a bend in the land. From past experience, she knew he'd be gone for at least thirty minutes.

She sprawled on a lounge chair and opened her

wrap to the morning sun. It was going to be another hot day, but at this early hour the heat was still pleasant. Closing her eyes, she enjoyed the peacefulness, and contemplated menu choices for the lunch they'd be serving later in the day.

They'd grill burgers—her own special blend with lots of garlic and Parmesan, and she'd make feta-cheese bundles for appetizers. When Kirk came back, she'd have to send him out to a produce stand for fresh lettuce and tomatoes and some fruit for dessert....

CLAIRE WAS ASLEEP on the lounge chair on the upper deck. Kirk paused momentarily, then walked closer. He was cool from his swim, and still wet. He'd forgotten to take a towel. Now he grabbed one of the girls' beach towels from the railing and used it to wipe the water from his back.

And all the while he watched Claire.

She was so beautiful and defenseless in her sleep. Her lovely hair was tousled, her thin cotton nightgown almost transparent in the sun. He was reminded of how she'd looked last Saturday morning when she'd awoken naked in their bed. He'd felt so hopeful then, especially after that fantastic breakfast they'd shared in bed.

Then he'd made that stupid phone call. And she'd assumed he was talking with Janice. He couldn't believe how much knowing that hurt. Did

Claire really believe he could make love to her so thoroughly, only to turn his back ten minutes later and phone another woman?

He'd felt they were on the road to healing. Then that had to happen.

"Are you really surprised?" he muttered as he hung the towel back on the railing. Wasn't her reaction exactly what he deserved?

Why *had* he done it? With each passing day his actions seemed more and more incredible to him. What had he been thinking? Sure he'd had fun with Janice, but was that fun worth the pain he'd caused Claire? The potential of splitting up his family? And his own resulting unhappiness?

Worse was the way he now felt about himself. As a kid, he'd been ashamed of his father for acting like a fool and leaving a wonderful wife to cavort with a woman twenty years younger. The aerobics instructor had hung around only long enough to get a reasonable divorce settlement, and his father had been alone after that. He'd died early, at sixty-two.

Kirk had loved his father, but he hadn't admired the way he'd chosen to live his life. Hadn't he himself consciously chosen another route?

Yet somehow he'd taken a similar wrong turn.

Was it too late? Was his future with Claire lost? Was starting a new life without her the only choice left to him?

Gazing down at his sleeping wife, Kirk knew he didn't want to start a new life. He wanted to stay with Claire, grow old with Claire. He wanted to be by her side when their kids graduated, then later when they married and had children. He wanted large family gatherings, and no arguments about whether Christmas would be with Mom or Dad this year.

And he'd do anything in his power to make it all happen. If he could, he'd rewrite the past, but since that wasn't possible, he'd offer the future.

If Claire gave him another chance, he'd never disappoint her again. How in hell, though, was he going to convince her of that?

Claire's head twisted to the side, out of the sun. A second later her eyes opened. Shielding her vision with an arm, she looked at him sleepily.

"Did you have a good swim?"

"Very good." He sat on the edge of the lounge chair, his hip lightly touching her thigh.

Through the gossamer cotton, he saw the shape of her breasts, the dark circles at their center. He sucked in air, then pushed his chest out with one deep breath. And forced himself to turn away.

Ripples glinted silver on the lake. The sky held just a tint of blue, like an aquamarine.

"I want you to trust me again, Claire." God but his mouth felt dry. "Do you think you ever could?"

Claire's eyelids lowered. She propped herself on her elbows. "You're asking for something you already had. I *did* trust you, Kirk. And look what happened."

"It was a mistake, Claire. Are you saying you can't give me another chance?" He was a fool to go out on a limb with a question like that, when the answer was sure to devastate him.

"Please, Claire." He took her hand and held it between both of his, all too aware of what he had to lose if she said no.

"I could try, Kirk. I *am* trying. It's just so hard." She pulled herself upright, leaving her hand in his.

"Fair enough." A chance. That was all he asked for.

GRADY ARRIVED at the Ridgeway cottage on his boat shortly before noon. Claire followed the rest of her family down to the dock, knowing that the girls were excited for the opportunity to do a little skiing and tubing.

Terese and Lisa arrived about twenty minutes later.

"We thought you'd be down here," Terese said, holding Lisa's hand as they descended the stairs that led from the back of the house to water level. "It's such a gorgeous day."

Terese was wearing a pair of shorts over her black bikini, and Lisa had on a darling pink sundress, which Claire recognized from Mallory's shop. Lisa was no sooner by the water's edge than she had that dress whipped over her head, revealing a two-piece suit much like her mom's.

"Can I ride in the boat?" she asked. "With the other girls?"

"Sure, sweetie," Terese said. "Just put your life jacket on so you'll be ready next time the boat comes round."

Claire patted the chair beside her for Terese, then reached into the cooler to offer her guest a choice of cold beverage.

Terese slipped out of her shorts before sitting down, the skin on her tummy barely wrinkling with the maneuver.

"Thanks, this is great." Terese popped the tab off an orange soda, took a swallow, then helped Lisa with the buckles on the life jacket. "Who's out there now?" she asked, casting a look to the lake.

"Kirk." He'd gotten up on one ski on his initial attempt. Pretty good for his first ski of the summer. "Andie's going to try next. She's thinking of dropping a ski."

Andie was sitting on the edge of the dock, her toes dipped in the water. Lisa plunked down next to her. "You're brave," she said. "That looks scary to me." She pointed at Kirk, who was poised at a forty-five-degree angle to the water, cutting a turn behind the wake of the boat as it headed back to shore.

Grady was at the wheel; Jenna and Daisy were acting as spotters at the back of the boat. The twins had plans with friends, Grady had told them, then winked and added *girl*friends.

"Just wait till it's your kids' turn," he'd said to Kirk, and Claire had been amused to see her husband's tan skin grow a little pale.

Now, as the boat traveled parallel to the dock, Kirk let go of the rope and sank into the lake. Grady cut the engine and cruised in closer.

"Hey, Terese," he called out with a friendly wave. "You made it. And there's Lisa. Coming in the boat, sweets?"

"You bet!" Lisa held out her hands, and when the boat was close enough, Grady scooped her into his arms.

Claire noticed Terese watching, a bittersweet expression on her face.

Meanwhile, Kirk had paddled back to the dock, his ski under one arm.

"Good ski, Dad," Andie said, leaning over the water to take the board from him.

"Thanks, it was fun." He laughed as he treaded water. He said hello to Terese, smiled at Claire, then faced his daughter. "Your turn, Andie."

"I know." She stepped down the ladder slowly. "Oh, it's so cold, Daddy."

Inside the boat, the three younger girls cheered as Andie struggled into the skis that Claire passed to Kirk. Kirk helped Andie get into position, holding her steady at the waist as Grady moved the boat forward to straighten the rope.

"I'll do one small circle, Andie," Grady called out, "then head back to the dock. That's when you should slip out of your ski if you plan to give it a try."

Claire slid forward to the edge of her seat. Andie wanted to do this so badly. *Please let her be successful.*

"Hit it!" Andie yelled, and the boat sprang ahead, towing her with it.

"She's up!" the younger girls called enthusiastically, and as promised, Grady took the boat for a fast jaunt before heading back to the dock.

Claire held her breath as Andie crouched down, releasing her left foot. The ski trailed behind, and it looked as though Andie was keeping her balance. Then—splash!—she went under, the rope flying ahead without her.

Claire was standing, her hands to her mouth. "Oh, Andie…"

Cutting powerful, quick strokes, Kirk swam out to his daughter. After a brief consultation he waved back to shore. "She's okay. She wants to try again."

And she did. A second time, then a third. Finally, she took a rest while Daisy had a ski, then the younger girls went for a tube ride.

On her fourth attempt, Andie managed to stay up for twenty seconds. On her fifth she tumbled headfirst into the water and came up gasping.

"That's enough," Claire told Kirk as he waited in the water. "She's got to be exhausted by now. I'm going inside to get lunch started. Everyone's probably starving."

Checking her watch, she realized it was already two-thirty. Good thing they'd had a big breakfast. She hoped her guests had, too.

Behind her she heard the boat come to shore, then Grady ask, "What about you, Terese? It's your turn now."

"I'm going to help Claire with lunch."

Claire paused while the other woman caught up with her. "Feel free to go for a ski," she said. "There's not that much to do in the kitchen."

"No, I want to help," Terese insisted.

Claire started the barbecue on the deck, then went inside to organize the fixings for burgers while Terese cut and buttered buns.

"Is everything okay, Terese?" she asked as she put out a dish of pickles. It seemed to her that Terese's expression was even more downcast than it had been yesterday.

"I suppose." Terese's shoulders rose, then sank, and she put a hand to her face. "Actually, not really. I had another phone call from Ed—my ex-husband.''

''Did he ask to see his daughter?''

''No. On that point, at least, I'm fortunate. I don't have to worry about sharing custody or visitation rights. Ed never did like to have anything to do with Lisa.''

''That's so sad.'' Claire patted Terese's shoulder. Shouldn't children bring a couple closer? That was what Claire had always thought. That was the way it had worked with her and Kirk.

Or so she'd always believed....

''I know, it *is* sad. But now I wish he'd just leave us alone. He wants me to come back to him, but when I reminded him of the restraining order, he got angry, and then I hung up.'' She shook her head. ''If it wasn't for having Lisa, I'd wish I'd never met him in the first place.''

''Did you tell the police about the call?''

''I phoned this morning. They said they'd give him a warning.'' Terese wiped away a tear, then reached for a tissue to blow her nose. ''I'm sorry. I shouldn't be bothering you with all this.''

''Please. If it helps to talk, I'm glad to listen.''

''My life must seem so strange to you. You have such a beautiful home, such a wonderful husband. And your girls are so cute.''

Yes, Claire reflected. That was her life. Or how it looked from the outside.

"I hope you don't mind that we invited Grady to lunch, too. It was Kirk's idea, but I don't want to make you uncomfortable."

Terese had washed her hands and was now back slicing buns. "It's no problem, Claire. I guess you know we were dating. When Ed turned up at my place, he and Grady got into such a terrible row. I didn't think it was fair to involve Grady in my problems. Especially since he has his sons to worry about. Not that I think Ed would hurt Warren and Taylor. But then, I never thought he would hurt Lisa or me, either."

"I can see your point." Claire put the feta-cheese appetizers she'd made earlier into the oven and pondered what Terese had said, how closely it mirrored her own opinion on the situation.

Only now, seeing Terese's vulnerability, she felt a stab of shame. The woman had been through a lot, was continuing to suffer. How long would she have to pay for her ex-husband's behavior?

Another one of those "no easy answer" situations. Claire sighed, then opened the fridge and pulled out the tray of burger patties.

"I'm going to put these on the grill."

When she came back, Terese was finished with the buns and was washing up the few dishes.

"I can't get the tap to stop dripping."

"I know." Claire pressed down on the handle,

to no avail. "I have to have that fixed.... Lisa sure seemed keen to try waterskiing."

"That kid is fearless." Terese's smile was half proud, half rueful. "And ever since she learned to talk, she's never hesitated to say exactly what's on her mind."

Claire thought of Andie. "Well, that can be a good thing."

"Sometimes. But it can also be embarrassing. Last week she told Grady she wanted him to be her daddy."

"Yes, well, kids say things like that."

"I'm just worried she's become too attached to him. Where would she have gotten an idea like that, do you think?"

"Well, Lisa's dad is out of the picture, and Grady is wonderful with kids..."

"I'll say." Terese used both hands to brush her short hair back from her face, then stood still for a moment. "It was a pleasure dealing with him when Warren and Taylor were having those problems at school. I wish all parents were willing to give their kids that much time and attention."

Claire considered Kirk, and his patience as he'd helped Andie in the water that morning. He'd never had as much time to spend with his children as Grady did, but when he was around, he was a good father.

Perhaps she'd been unfair all these years to expect more. Kirk never could have achieved his success as a stockbroker if he'd worked the hours that Grady did. She would willingly trade some of that success for his spending more time with the children. But that choice was Kirk's to make.

CHAPTER EIGHTEEN

"WHAT DO YOU THINK it would take to get you to trust Kirk again?" Riva Sharp asked Claire during her counseling session that Tuesday.

Riva had requested that Claire and Kirk come to her separately for a few weeks. To deal with a few of their own issues. Claire was impatient with the idea. Wasn't the point to work on the marriage? Didn't they need to be together for that to happen?

"I'm not sure, Riva," she said, smoothing down the front of her sundress. Her belly was expanding daily now, a constant reminder of the new life developing inside her.

Her doctor in Toronto had made arrangements with a general practitioner here in Barrie, and Claire had a doctor's appointment after her session with Riva. Claire would have been happy to skip the monthly appointments—she'd sailed through her first three pregnancies and saw no reason to worry about this one—but her doctor had convinced her.

"You'll need to get some blood work done,"

he'd said. "Plus at your age you really should consider an amniocentesis."

That had been a month ago. Somehow she still hadn't broached the subject with Kirk, even though she knew the risks for certain abnormalities such as Down's syndrome and spina bifida were higher for women over age thirty-five.

But what pressed more on her mind was whether this child would be born into a happy family—or a newly divided one.

"Have you given the matter of trust any thought?"

"Well, of course I've given it thought." That didn't mean she'd come to any resolution.

Riva leaned back in her chair and slipped half glasses from her face.

"How is Kirk generally? Does he flirt when he's around other women? Is he secretive about where he's going and what he's doing? In other words, is this thing with his co-worker an aberration? Or is it part of a pattern of behavior?"

"An aberration," Claire said quickly. Then realized what the counselor had so cleverly accomplished. She laughed dryly and finally had to tip her hat to the woman across from her.

"I see where you're going with this. You think Kirk deserves a second chance."

"I can't say what's right for another person. Everyone has her limit to what she can and cannot live with. If you're going to stay married, you don't have to forgive Kirk, but you do have to get past this thing with the co-worker. You have to see it for what it is. An anomaly."

"That sounds so logical. Especially when I think about my children...."

Riva nodded.

"But it's hard." Claire told her about the phone call the morning after she and Kirk had made love. "I don't want to spend my life wondering what my husband is saying and doing when I'm not around. The thing is, the next time I walk in on him talking on the phone, I'm not sure I won't have the exact same reaction."

"I understand completely, Claire. Would it help if I told you that trust does return? Gradually, I'll admit. And only if both parties are working hard to repair the damage."

"Please don't tell me an affair can make a marriage stronger. I've read that in some of the literature, and I'm sorry, but I don't buy it."

"Not the affair itself," Riva agreed. "But the self-examination that follows it." She slipped her glasses on once more, checked her notes, then looked at Claire again.

"Think back several years, Claire. Say, to when your youngest daughter was three or four. What was your marriage like then? Were you completely satisfied with it? Do you think Kirk was?"

Oh, that was a tough one. Claire leaned forward, covering her face with her hands. Two or three years ago...

"Not completely satisfied, no..." she admitted, wishing she could say otherwise. "Kirk's long hours at work were always a point of contention between us. Often, I..."

"Yes?"

Claire had been about to say that she'd sometimes wondered if she'd made a mistake in marrying Kirk. An ambitious, successful businessman might seem a wonderful catch to many women, yet occasionally she'd wondered what her life would have been like if things had worked out differently between her and Grady.

But what did any of that have to do with Kirk's relationship with Janice? With her ability to trust him again?

Claire scanned the now-familiar room—the crowded bookshelves, the tidy desk, the open window. She thought of her children, the way they'd all laughed that morning when Jenna had put a dollop of Kirk's shaving cream on her hair by mistake, thinking it was mousse. She thought of her parents, and their habit of holding hands whenever they walked together. And she thought of Kirk, how he'd caught and held her gaze when he'd said goodbye.

"You were saying..." Riva prompted.

Claire blinked, and looked back at the counselor. What had they been talking about? Her thoughts had fragmented.

"I'm not sure," she said. "I'm just not sure."

"How did things go?" Mallory asked later in the afternoon when Claire arrived to pick up the kids. She was standing at the kitchen table, folding a load of Angel's clean clothes.

"Not bad." Claire set her purse down on the counter and went to the table to help. She picked up a T-shirt and smoothed out the wrinkles with her hand.

"We talked about trust." She sighed. The session with Riva Sharp had unsettled her, as usual, and she wasn't ready to talk about it. "Then I went to my appointment with the doctor."

"And? How was everything? Is the baby okay?"

"Just fine. Fetal heart rate is normal. My weight gain is within the accepted range—so far—and my blood pressure is excellent, too."

The doctor had also pressed her to make an appointment for her amnio as soon as possible. Regardless of the results of the triple-screen blood test they'd taken, he was recommending the procedure.

"No time to lose," he stressed. "You're in your seventeenth week."

Claire scribbled a mental note to discuss the procedure with Kirk when he called her that evening.

"I saw the girls in the backyard as I was coming in. Did they behave themselves for you?"

"They've been fine, keeping Angel amused while I catch up on the laundry from our weekend in Ottawa. Why do people always go through more clothing when they're on vacation than when they're at home?"

"Tell me about it. I definitely spend more time at the washing machine than I do on the deck when we're at the cottage. The girls change about three times a day. Then there are all those beach towels... By the way, how *was* your holiday?"

"Lovely. I'm glad Drew decided not to sell his place. It's so beautiful in the Gatineaus, Claire."

Having finished the last of Angel's clothing, Mallory put the laundry basket down on the floor. "One more thing I should probably mention..."

"Yes?"

"Andie asked if Drew and I slept in the same bed when I was pregnant with Angel."

"Oh?" Claire thought about the blankets on the couch whenever Kirk came up for the weekend. "Oh!"

"I take it you and Kirk...?"

Claire rubbed her forehead with her palm. "The counselor said we should try to keep life normal for the sake of the children. But sleeping together... So far I haven't been able to do it.''

Except for that one night in Toronto, which had been so wonderful. Until Kirk made that phone call. Claire had done a lot of thinking about that, not to mention discussing the situation with Riva.

Perhaps she'd been too suspicious. But when she'd heard his voice, warm and low—and especially that word, *sorry*—her mind had automatically jumped to Janice.

''What did you tell Andie when she asked the question?''

''That sometimes pregnant women sleep alone if they're feeling uncomfortable.''

Yes, some pregnant women did. She never had, though. Until now. And the reasons she and Kirk slept apart had nothing to do with her pregnancy. But Claire didn't want her daughter to know that.

THAT EVENING, after the younger children were in bed, Claire asked Andie if she'd like to play Monopoly. Andie pulled out the old board game and set the pieces up on the kitchen end of the pine table.

''You be the banker,'' Claire said.

''Just trying to get me to do more math, aren't you?''

''You bet.'' Claire got a plate of brownies and two large glasses of milk for them to snack on as they played. The game had been going on for more than an hour, when the phone rang.

Claire glanced at the card she'd just pulled from the stack at the center of the board. "Oh, no. I have to go to jail again." She moved her marker to the corner square, then went to the phone. "Hello?"

"Claire."

Kirk's voice rumbled in her ear, and even though she'd been expecting to hear from him, she felt her heart pound in her chest.

"How did your session go today?"

Claire reflected on her hour with Riva. Why did she always feel so ambiguous about their conversations?

"I guess it went okay." Finding out that some people were able to trust again after going through experiences like hers and Kirk's had been encouraging. Now the big question was whether she would be one of those people.

"That's good. And the appointment with the doctor?"

"That went well, too." Claire thought about the amniocentesis, but she didn't want to discuss it with Andie listening. It would only give her daughter one more thing to worry about.

"Great! I go for my appointment with Riva tomorrow. If you want I'll call..."

"Yes," she said quickly. "That would be fine, but later."

"When the kids are in bed? So we can talk?"

"Exactly."

"Speaking of which, how are they doing? Did they have a fun day at Mallory's?"

"Yes. They played so hard they were exhausted when I got them home. Jenna fell asleep at the dinner table and Daisy wasn't far behind her. Andie's still up, whipping me at Monopoly. Do you want to speak with her?"

Andie took the phone. "Hi, Daddy. She's letting me win, as usual."

Claire pretended to look surprised. *Who? Me?* she mouthed, which made Andie smile.

Claire smiled back, but in reality she felt a little sad. When, exactly, had her daughter learned to see through her so easily?

THE NEXT MORNING, Kirk strode off the elevator toward the curved cherry-wood desk where Tara, the receptionist, was speaking on the phone. She smiled and held out his copy of the *National Post*.

"Thanks, Tara." He glanced at the headline. Bad news about the unemployment rate. With a twist of his hand, he opened the door to the secured area, walked past the cage where traders would be processing market transactions in about an hour, then followed the corridor to his large corner office.

The trappings of success. His personal assistant, Greer, who'd be bringing in his coffee any moment; an expensively appointed office, with sofa, chairs and coffee table for entertaining clients and a hell of a view of Lake Ontario—if you overlooked the sea of office towers that came before it.

True, there was that empty space on the wall opposite him—the abstract he'd bought a few months ago hadn't suited him after all—but he'd fill the gap soon. He was thinking of having a family photograph taken after the baby was born.

Assuming they were still a family then....

Kirk turned on his computer and was just logging on when Greer came in with his coffee.

"Good morning."

"Thanks, Greer." She whisked in and out so fast all he caught was a blur of floral fabric and a whiff of her perfume. But there was his mug, on the ceramic coaster Andie had made for Father's Day when she was in grade one. He reached for the handle automatically as the Starquotes from the Toronto Stock Exchange came up on his screen.

He sipped the coffee. Hot, strong, freshly brewed. Full points to Greer, as usual.

First Kirk checked the current bid and ask prices on a stock he'd purchased for several of his clients yesterday. Up ten cents. Well, that was a good sign the price would climb, even though the market wouldn't be open until nine-thirty. He glanced at his watch. In another forty-five minutes.

After removing his reading glasses from his breast pocket, he slipped them on, then breezed through the paper while he finished his coffee. Fifteen minutes later, he listened to his voice-mail messages.

Generally, he loved this first hour of the day, before the markets opened and the flood of client phone calls began. He needed the time to clear his mind, to focus on the priorities of the day. More and more, administrative matters and office politics were intruding on his work. Natural fallout from the kind of success he'd earned in his many years with the firm.

Here, everyone valued his opinion; his business acumen had won him respect and admiration. Aware of the natural pitfalls of being a stockbroker, he'd consciously steered clear of trouble in his career, often walking away from situations offering a quick profit when he sensed the underlying economics were suspect.

The result was a reputation for integrity *and* acumen. He'd worked hard to earn it. He just wished that it meant a damn to Claire.

She seemed to take their healthy income, their substantial investment portfolio for granted. As for the work he did, she rarely asked questions and never focused long when he brought the subject up. If he told her about a great deal he'd closed, she usually said something like ''That's great, Kirk. Do you think you could come by Daisy's school for her dance recital tomorrow at three?''

In her eyes he was a failure. Because he couldn't always make it for those recitals, parent-teacher interviews and student performances, which she structured her life around.

Kirk picked up a framed photo of the three girls shot last Christmas. Lord, how he missed them. He couldn't remember feeling this lonely other summers. Maybe because other years he hadn't been facing the possibility of losing them forever.

Except for every other weekend and a couple weeks' holiday each year.

It wouldn't be enough. Even on those nights that he came home too late to tuck them in, he slept better knowing they were all under the same roof. They were a family. And, by God, he wanted to do everything in his power to keep them that way.

''Kirk?''

Startled, he propped the photo back on his desk and looked up. Janice. Oh, hell.

''How are you doing?'' she asked, closing the door and leaning back against it.

She was tanned from her holiday and had on a navy dress with a deep vee neck, and impossibly high heels. The kind Claire claimed had been invented to hobble women so they couldn't run away from the men they attracted by wearing those shoes.

"I'm fine, Janice. You?" They hadn't spoken since she'd come back to work. He stood and went to open the door.

She looked at him questioningly, and he thought about what he and the marriage counselor had talked about yesterday.

"Do you love your wife, Kirk?" she'd asked him.

No question he did.

"Then you've got to earn back her trust."

"Yes. But how?"

She'd nailed him with that levelheaded look of hers. "By being trustworthy."

Yes. It was that simple. And that complicated.

"I don't think Claire would appreciate us talking in here with the door closed," he said now, explaining his action to Janice.

"I don't get this," she said in a hushed voice, her eyes lowering defensively. "I know you said things had to change between us. But what about our friendship? I've come to really count on you, Kirk. And I miss our time together."

"We can't be friends anymore, Janice. It wouldn't be right."

"But why?"

Did she really not get it? "Claire has to come

first. She's my wife, after all. I wouldn't blame her for being angry at seeing us together." He stepped back to his desk. "I think you ought to go back to work, Janice."

"You are a heartless bastard."

The feeling behind the words gave him a quiver of conscience. He hadn't meant to hurt Janice. Perhaps he could have been kinder. Perhaps he could have softened the blow. But instinct told him blunt honesty was the only way. And the sound of Claire's sobs was now indelibly etched in his conscience.

"I'm sorry if you're unhappy. But the mistake I made, the mistake we both made, was in letting our friendship get out of hand in the first place. Calling it quits now is the only right thing to do. For both of us. You need to meet a man who can give you his whole heart. That's what you deserve, Janice. And I need to think of my wife."

Janice flinched at the word *wife,* then stepped forward until she was close enough that he could hear her whisper. "I can't keep working at this firm if we aren't together."

He looked down at his desk, at the blotter that protected the smooth, polished wood. Janice leaving was the best thing he could hope for. It would help give Claire peace of mind that the affair was truly over. Still, he couldn't ask her to quit.

"That's your decision," he said finally.

Janice leaned in closer. "Is that all you have to say?"

He didn't even have to think. "Absolutely."

CHAPTER NINETEEN

"JUST A WORN-OUT WASHER," Grady said, leaning over Claire's kitchen sink.

The constant plip-plop from the faucet had been driving her crazy all week, but she'd been waiting for Kirk to come home to fix it. She was really anxious for him to arrive—had been since the phone call this afternoon with the results of her blood test.

But of course he wouldn't be here for hours. And by then Grady would have the faucet repaired.

"I noticed this dripping during lunch last weekend," he said, unscrewing the top. "It will take only a minute to replace." He knelt by his toolbox, searched for a few moments, then stood, shaking his head. "Must have left those washers in the Jeep. I'll just be a sec."

Claire got a cold beer out of the fridge and opened it for Grady. She paused when she caught Andie staring up from her math workbook. She'd been on her second page for the day but had dropped her pencil the minute Grady walked to the door. So far she hadn't picked it up again, even though Grady had tried to tease her into it.

"What time will Daddy be here?"

Claire didn't need to check the clock. "You know he usually doesn't arrive until after dark, hon. When you and your sisters are already asleep."

Andie scowled, but before Claire could ask what was wrong, Grady had returned. She heard him stomp on the outside mat, then he pushed the door open.

"Found just what I need. And, Andie?" He grinned at the girl who hadn't spared him so much as a smile since he'd walked in fifteen minutes ago. "I think I hear your dad's car driving down the lane."

"Really?" Andie pushed back her chair and rushed out. Daisy and Jenna, who'd been playing with Barbie dolls by the patio doors, were right behind her.

Claire shrugged apologetically at Grady for her daughter's rudeness, then looked at her wrist. Only five-thirty. Kirk must have left work very early. She glanced into the mirror on the wall by the door and noted the pink in her cheeks. Her heart was pounding ridiculously fast for a woman about to greet a man she'd been married to for over a decade.

What was the big deal?

But having him home so early on a Friday was such a treat. He must have missed them. Or maybe just the girls...

"Go on," Grady teased. "Run out the door and say hello. I can see you're dying to."

"I'll let the girls have the first chance. Hopefully, he'll still be standing once they've finished their ambush." Claire pushed her hair behind her ears, then peered over the ledge that acted as a mini backsplash to the sink and inspected his work.

"Is that the old screen?" she asked, spying a flat circular disk on the counter.

"Yeah. All plugged up. You definitely needed a new one, so I replaced both it and the washer." With nimble fingers, Grady began to screw the tap back together just as the front door was flung open.

Kirk stood alone in the doorway, still wearing his suit from the office. He leveled his eyes at Claire, and right away she knew something was wrong.

Claire straightened and looked behind him. "Where are the girls?"

There was a dangerous stillness to Kirk's expression as he closed the door deliberately behind him. Not just the screen door but the wooden one, too.

He didn't answer her question, just dropped his weekend bag, then took a few steps forward.

Claire's feeling of unease escalated. Why was

he ignoring Grady? He must have seen the Jeep out front, and by now he would have noticed Grady standing by the sink in the kitchen.

But his gaze focused on her as though she were the only one in the room. And still he didn't talk.

Feeling awkward, Claire began to chatter. "Grady stopped on his way home from work to fix the faucet. Won't it be nice not to have to listen to that stupid dripping all the time?"

"I could have fixed it," Kirk said finally, taking another couple of steps. All of a sudden Claire was glad the counter separated the two men. She recognized the granite edge to Kirk's dark gray eyes now. He was about to lose his cool. It didn't happen often, but when it did...

"Hey," Grady said, flashing a smile. "I'm sure you could, Kirk. But it was no trouble for me to come out here. After all, it's only a few miles."

"True," Kirk said. "Makes me wonder, though. How many times a week do you generally drop in to visit my wife?"

Claire's mouth went slack. Now she was the one who couldn't find words. Did Kirk realize what he was implying?

"Come on, Kirk." There was a cautious note behind Grady's good-humored tone. "What's gotten into you?"

As Grady stepped out from behind the kitchen counter, Claire moved forward quickly. She had a feeling she'd better keep these two apart. She turned to Kirk, hoping he'd realize how ridiculously he was behaving.

"Grady's a good friend. He and his sons are welcome here anytime. Right?"

She looked at Kirk, waiting for him to confirm the invitation. Whatever weirdness had gotten into him today, he needed to get it under control. And quick.

But she wasn't encouraged by the sardonic expression that glimmered in his eyes as he spoke. "Oh, sure, Claire. Grady's so good with kids, so handy with repairs. I see why you'd want to have him around. Maybe even more than your husband."

"What?" She'd never heard Kirk talk this way before. It was crazy, and embarrassing.... She eyed Grady, shaking her head apologetically.

"I don't know what's up, Kirk," he said. "You know I think the world of Claire, but you can't seriously believe there's anything going on..."

"Oh?" Kirk stepped sideways, blocking Grady's path. "Can't I?"

"Hell." Grady glanced back at Claire, who was too overwhelmed to speak, then swore again, more softly. "Maybe things'd be a lot clearer if I made a little confession."

Kirk's chin rose a notch. "That sounds like a good idea."

"I *am* in love, Kirk. So much that I can hardly think straight. And I sure as hell can't sleep at night. But I'm not in love with Claire. It's Terese."

For the first time, hesitation sparked in Kirk's eyes, and Grady pushed his advantage.

"Couldn't you tell how I felt about her last weekend? It was pretty obvious."

Kirk regarded the two of them, measuring, calculating. After a moment, the hard set of his mouth eased and he backed away from the door.

"Yeah. I noticed." He met Grady's gaze. "I guess I was out of line."

"That's okay. You've been under pressure. Believe me, I understand." Grady patted Kirk on the shoulder as he headed for the door. Before leaving, he looked back at Claire.

"Thanks for the beer."

Claire was so embarrassed she could hardly meet his eyes. "Thanks f-for the faucet...."

When the door had closed, Claire turned to her husband, her embarrassment flaring into anger. Grady was a good guy; he probably wouldn't hold this against Kirk. But she wasn't as forgiving. Her hands tightened into fists, and she took a deep breath, hardly knowing where to start.

"That was *insane*, Kirk."

To her great consternation, Kirk didn't look the slightest bit abashed. He threw his overnight bag on the couch, then faced her, hands on his hips, feet planted shoulder-width apart.

"Was it?" he said, his tone as hard as the expression on his face.

Claire had never felt frightened of her husband before. Now, for the first time, she did, and the emotion had a bitter, ugly tang. "Why would you think Grady and I—"

"Why?" The word blasted from Kirk's mouth. "Have you ever asked yourself how you feel about Grady? How you *really* feel. 'Cause from where I stand you practically worship the guy. If you had half the admiration for me that you have for him…"

Kirk strode to the fireplace, where he picked up the poker and slashed at the cold ashes. "Grady's such a wonderful father, such a model husband. Always home for dinner, always there to help with the kids. Isn't that what you really want, Claire? Isn't it true that I've been a big disappointment to you?"

She was blown away by the ruthlessness of his conclusion. "That's not a fair comparison."

"Maybe not." Kirk withdrew the poker, allowed it to hang by his side. "But you're the one who's always making it. Why did you marry me in the first place? You knew I was ambitious. You knew what I wanted."

Yes, she'd known, and admired him for it.

"I was second choice, wasn't I? You really wanted Grady, but he was already married to Bess. Isn't that a fact, Claire?"

"This is ridiculous." Claire wanted to put her hands over her ears. "If you think you can deflect attention from your affair by pointing a finger at me..."

She whirled around and headed for the bedroom, but paused at the end of the hall. "I have never been unfaithful to you."

"Is that right?" Kirk threw down the poker, and Claire winced as it thudded on the pine floor. "Maybe not in deed," he said.

Anger buzzed in Claire's head. She couldn't think anymore she was so *furious*. "Don't try to twist this on me. You're the one who had an affair. You're the one who broke our wedding vows. *You fell in love with her.*"

"And aren't you still in love with Grady? Even just a little?"

"No." She turned her back. He couldn't talk to her this way. She didn't deserve—

"I admit what I did was wrong," Kirk said, his voice quieter, but somehow colder for it. "But at least I've made an effort to be honest. Maybe it's time you did the same."

KIRK WAS WRONG, WRONG, WRONG! She wasn't in love with Grady. Sure, she had a soft spot for him.

Wasn't that normal? Didn't most women feel that way about their first love?

Claire paced the length of her bedroom, pausing to punch some air in her pillows, before pacing some more. Ten minutes later she heard a tentative knock.

"Leave your mother alone. She's resting." Kirk's voice growled from somewhere in the main living area of the cottage. Whoever was at the door retreated.

After half an hour, Claire was beginning to feel like a caged animal. But she couldn't go out; she was too afraid of starting a scene in front of their daughters. Eventually, she heard some sounds in the kitchen, then the smell of cooking. Eggs, maybe? And something else....

There was a second knock on her door. Claire opened it and found Andie with a tray of food: creamed eggs on waffles; a cup of tea, with a sliced lemon on the saucer.

"You'd better eat this," Andie ordered. "Dad went to a lot of trouble for you."

Claire couldn't meet her daughter's eyes. "Thank you, Andie."

After the door closed, Claire sat on the edge of her bed with the tray on her knees. Her gut was still burning with anger and pain; eating seemed impossible. Yet she didn't dare return the tray with the food untouched.

The first bite was a struggle, but the meal went down more easily than she would have thought. This baby wanted to be fed, she decided, regardless of the state of its mother's mental health. Claire shook off the thought of those damn blood tests. Her baby was normal. She just knew it.

The tea was soothing against the rawness of her throat. Claire cupped the mug with both hands and tried to focus on pleasant, calming things. She imagined she was floating on the lake, rising and falling with the gentle swell of the waves. Soon, her trembling stopped and her anxiety eased. By the time she'd finished the tea, a measure of equanimity had returned. She crawled under the covers and sleep came quickly.

When she awoke, it was morning. The room was hot, the air still, and her head felt like a stone. She glanced around, noticed the tray from last night had been removed, then closed her eyes to rest for another minute—and fell back asleep. About an hour later she woke again, this time with her head feeling a little lighter.

She pulled on maternity shorts and a new hand-painted T-shirt from Mallory's shop. When she opened the bedroom door it was to a quiet, deserted house. A note was propped up against the faucet.

The *nondripping* faucet.

Claire, we've gone waterskiing with the Hogans. Andie wants to try dropping a ski again. Don't worry about dinner. I'll make it when I get home.

Kirk

Claire stared at her husband's signature, then re-read the note. There was certainly no sign of any regret in those brief sentences for the previous day's argument. But he was going out on the boat with Grady. That meant he must have called and apologized for yesterday's scene. She intended to add her own apology in short order.

However, there was someone else she needed to see first.

Claire baked a double batch of her family's favorite cookies, then had two, plus some fruit salad and a glass of milk, for breakfast. When she was finished and the kitchen tidy once more, she packaged up the cookies, then grabbed the keys to the van.

So much had gone haywire this summer it seemed an impossible task to sort everything out. But if her marriage to Kirk was going down the drain, she wasn't about to pull any other happy relationships along with it.

Driving down the tree-lined lane, she thought of the desperate sincerity in Grady's voice when he'd said *I love Terese.*

She'd been such a bloody fool about that relationship. This was no transitional affair, and Grady wasn't simply acting the part of hero to the rescue. He truly cared about the petite woman, and Claire was certain that Terese loved him equally in return.

In twelve minutes she was in Port Carling and parked out front of the Conroys' pretty Victorian-style house. Terese and Lisa were still living in the basement apartment; she hoped she'd find them at home.

The midmorning sun was warm on her back and her head as Claire walked along the stone steps that led to the backyard. Woolly thyme grew wild in the dirt spaces between the stones, and with each step she released some of the familiar scent into the air.

She found Terese sitting on the deck, sketching something in the grass by her feet. One of the straps from her baggy overalls had fallen off her shoulder, and her bangs were clipped back from her face, revealing a smooth, slightly rounded forehead.

Terese's concentration was so intense Claire hesitated to intrude. Then abruptly Terese looked up, one dark eyebrow rising in a dramatic arch. "Hello, Claire."

Claire stepped closer, then bent to examine the fragile blue, bell-shaped wildflower that Terese was replicating on paper. "I didn't mean to interrupt. Where's Lisa?"

"Playing at a friend's." Terese added a line to her drawing, then snapped the pad closed. "I'm glad you stopped by. I needed a break. Why don't you sit down." She indicated a second chair, which shared the shade of an old maple. "Could I offer you a cool drink?"

Claire relaxed deep into the seat and let out a sigh. "That would be nice."

Terese disappeared inside and came out with two glasses of lemonade. Claire had a long swallow of the refreshingly cold beverage and smiled her thanks. "Kirk's taken the girls out for the day. I feel a little at loose ends."

"Still, it's nice to have a break, isn't it? Much as I adore Lisa, the constant stream of conversation gets to me sometimes. Especially when I'm trying to draw or paint."

"It's the age," Claire assured her. "Five-year-olds will recount their life story to a parking attendant if he stands still long enough. It's a cute stage, really. Just wait until she turns ten and won't tell you what she's thinking anymore."

Andie. That accusing look from yesterday was fresh in her memory, and still had the power to wound. For some reason Andie seemed to blame *her* because Kirk wasn't around as much as Andie would like. *If you were nicer to him...* Her daughter's words came back to Claire, along with Kirk's accusation of the previous day: *Aren't you still in love with Grady?*

"It's good to be reminded how quickly they grow up. I can't believe Lisa starts school full-time this September."

"And Jenna next year."

"Isn't letting go hard?" Terese said. She settled her head against the back of the chair and stared up into the canopy of maple leaves. "Just think how Grady must feel with the twins about to start their last year of high school."

"Speaking of Grady..." Claire leaned forward in her chair. This was, after all, why she had come. "Have you seen him lately?"

Terese sighed. "Not since lunch at your place the long weekend."

A light breeze carried perfume from Pat Conroy's rose garden. Claire heard the leaves whisper around her. "Maybe you should. See him, I mean."

Terese's eyes opened wide. "When we talked the other day, I got the distinct impression you agreed with me that it wasn't a good idea to drag him and his boys into my—my situation."

Claire shook her head. "That was so wrong of me. I was just being—oh, I don't know. Overprotective? I've always had a soft spot for Grady, and I want him to be happy."

"Me, too," Terese said quietly.

"Being with you makes him happy, Terese."

The petite woman smiled uncertainly. "But my ex-husband—"

"How long since you left him?"

"Almost three years."

"Then isn't it time he stopped controlling your life? You deserve happiness, Terese. So does Grady." And what if Ed turned out to be one of those psychos who showed up one night with a hatchet and an intent to kill?

Okay, not a likely scenario. But the fact that the man was Lisa's father meant he would always be a part of Terese's life. And everyone agreed he had the potential for violence. Yet that was hardly Terese's fault. Besides, Grady loved Terese.

"I just don't know what Ed is capable of," Terese said. "That's what really scares me."

"Understandably. But you can't let him block the happiness you so obviously find with Grady."

Terese ran her hands through her thick dark hair, her expression an agony of indecision. "Don't you think that would be selfish of me? Putting my own happiness above the safety of Grady and his boys?"

For Claire to admit what she knew was true was hard. "Grady and the boys can look after themselves."

Terese laughed without humor. "That's what Grady says."

"Then believe him." Claire leaned forward to touch the little wildflower poking up from the grass. "And love him. That's what I'd do."

CHAPTER TWENTY

DREW'S EXPLORER, as well as Kirk's sedan, were parked outside Grady's home. Claire wasn't surprised. Mallory worked at her boutique on Saturdays, so it made sense that Drew would bring Angel to hang out at Grady's.

No point in knocking at the front door; they wouldn't be inside on a great day like this. She picked up the box of cookies from the floor of the van, then headed around the house to the gray deck that connected house to boathouse. A thirty-foot pier ran perpendicular to the deck, branching out into a T at the end. That was where she saw Grady, his attention on the lake.

Boards creaked and Claire's thongs snapped against the wood as she walked out to meet him. He was sitting on a deck chair, his wet hair plastered against his head, droplets of water still clinging to his powerful back and shoulders. Tumbled at his feet was a collection of beach towels, two bottles of sunscreen and a single water ski.

He twisted around when he heard her approach and raised a hand in friendly salute. "Claire. Perfect timing. Daisy's skiing right now, and when she's done, Andie's going to try dropping her ski.''

Claire's gaze shot out to the water. She could just make out the red-and-white of Grady's motorboat and the small dot that was her daughter, being pulled behind. ''Who's driving?''

''Drew. Kirk's in the boat, too, along with all the kids.''

At the mention of her husband's name, her eyes caught Grady's and held them for a few moments. ''About last night—''

Grady shook his head. ''Don't say a word. We men have sorted everything out.''

''Are you sure? I can't tell you how mortified I feel…. I still can't believe he said those things.''

''You've got to cut the guy some slack. He's been under a lot of pressure.'' Grady's usually good-humored face set into bleak lines. ''It's a scary thing for a man to face the prospect of his family breaking up. Believe me, I know.''

''Still. It *was* kind of ridiculous.''

''Ridiculous?'' Grady's eyebrows rose. ''Kirk knows you and I have a history. I could see how a man might be threatened by our friendship.''

Claire sat in the chair next to him, feeling the dock sway under her. The boat was out of sight now and she focused on the man beside her. ''Yes, but our history lies almost twenty years in the past. We were just kids.''

Yet even as she spoke the words, her mind was telling her a different story. *Come on, Claire. Maybe your feelings for Grady aren't truly in the past.*

She shut her mouth and looked out to the water. What *were* her feelings for the man beside her? If she was going to be honest with Kirk, she needed to start by being truthful with herself.

The memory of her last counseling session loomed, in particular the moment Riva had asked about Claire and Kirk's marriage in the years before Janice.

She'd admitted to Riva that even then there had been problems, and right after admitting that she'd thought of Grady, although she hadn't said anything. What did that indicate about her commitment to Kirk and to their marriage? She couldn't blame Kirk for accusing her of comparing him with Grady and finding him short of the mark, when it was true. And not just since the affair with Janice, but years before.

Beginning, she acknowledged, when the demands of family life had started to impinge on Kirk's career. That was when she'd begun to suffer the occasional stab of doubt. *Had she married the right man?*

"Yeah, it's been a lot of years," Grady conceded. "But you have to know the way the male mind operates. This is going to sound arrogant, but a man likes to feel that as far as his woman is concerned, he's the one and only.''

''An interesting point. How do you think women want to feel? That they're one out of five?''

Grady laughed. ''Hell, Claire, you don't give an inch, do you? The point I'm trying to make is that the male ego is *fragile*. And believe me, after my divorce, I know of what I speak.''

''Oh, Grady.'' She reached out to touch his arm. ''You are such a great guy.''

''I appreciate the sentiment. But your husband needs to hear those words from you.''

Claire sat back in her chair, stung.

''Hey. I didn't intend to sound ungracious. Your friendship means a lot to me, Claire. And it's exactly why I'm being so blunt. Whatever problems you two are facing right now, sort them out. You and Kirk don't want to end up like me and Bess. And there's no reason you should. You guys are great together, and you've manufactured three super kids.'' He glanced at her belly.

She knew what he was thinking. *Soon to be four.* Protectively, she wrapped her arms around her middle. She'd started feeling the baby's movements a couple of weeks ago. And those first flutters had awoken her maternal instincts with a vengeance.

She loved this baby. She wanted this baby. Regardless of what happened between Kirk and her.

"I hear you, Grady. But I still have a hard time taking Kirk's insecurities seriously. After all, I'm obviously pregnant. As if any man would be interested in me now."

"I guess I'd have to disagree with you on that one. But the point is, you and Kirk belong together. And I'm...well, you know how I feel about Terese. I'd marry her in a flash if she'd have me. But she's so spooked by her ex-husband..."

Guilt forced Claire's gaze down to the boards of the dock. Only too recently she'd thought the same way. "Is he dangerous, Grady? *Really* dangerous?"

"I don't know. But the fact that he's out there only makes me love Terese more. Maybe because I feel she needs me."

"That fragile-male-ego thing again?"

Grady gave her chair a kick. "Offer a woman a little inside information, and she turns on you."

Claire smiled. "I'm not turning on you, Grady. I really do hope you and Terese work things out."

"Here comes the boat." Grady pointed to a speck in the distance.

As they watched, the speck grew bigger, and eventually took on shape and color. Within a minute Claire could make out Drew at the wheel and Kirk behind.

"Can you see who's skiing?"

"I think it's Andie."

A few seconds later Claire could discern the red of her daughter's hair. The boat was still coming in their direction; in about one minute it would be parallel to the dock. Which was when Andie would slip her left foot out of her ski and try to keep her balance on the remaining one.

Grady stood and started shouting instructions. "Not yet, Andie." A few seconds passed. "Okay, bend down, get ready…"

Then, just a split second before the boat whizzed by, Grady raised his hand. "Now!"

On cue, Andie kicked off her left ski, wobbled to the right, straightened, then wobbled to the left—

"Come on, Andie!" Claire cheered.

—then stabilized in the center.

"She's doing it, Grady! She's actually doing it!" Claire was so glad for her daughter. She'd had such a tough summer. At least this one thing had gone right.

"Sure she is. She's one determined kid."

They watched until the boat had circled out of sight, with Andie still balancing on her single ski. Then Grady sat back in his chair and glanced at the package Claire had stowed under her chair.

"Now, tell me what's in that container, or I'm going to have to throw you into the lake."

Claire pulled her sunglasses from the top of her

head to the bridge of her nose. Smiling, she just shook her head. "Be patient."

Grady groaned. "You can be cruel, you know that? I'll bet they're those Triple Temptation Cookies, aren't they?"

"You'll just have to wait and see."

AFTER ANDIE'S successful circuit on one ski, the boat headed for home.

"Hey, Claire!" Drew waved from the front seat after cutting the throttle. "Did you see your daughter?"

"I sure did. That was terrific, hon!" She waved at Andie, who was breast-stroking toward the other end of the pier.

Grady grabbed for the side of the boat as it came near and pulled it in gently to rest alongside the wooden platform. With practiced ease he secured the boat while Claire helped Kirk unload the children and Andie hauled herself out of the lake.

"That was fantastic, kiddo," Kirk said, wrapping a big towel around Andie's body. She was shivering like crazy, but her lips were stretched into the biggest smile.

"It was so much fun, Daddy! Did you see me, Mom?"

"I sure did." Claire turned and gave the towel around Andie a brisk rub. "You had great balance out there, hon." She glanced up at Kirk and felt her smile stiffen. When he looked at her there were questions in his eyes she wasn't sure how to answer.

Maybe she'd made some mistakes in the past. Maybe she'd done too much comparing, and maybe it hadn't been fair. But that didn't justify what Kirk had done. No matter what her dissatisfactions with the marriage, she'd never gone behind Kirk's back to find her pleasure elsewhere.

"Did you see me ski, Mommy?" Daisy asked.

Claire bent to kiss the tip of the nose visible from behind Daisy's flower-shaped sunglasses. "I saw a little. Did you have trouble getting up?"

"Nope. Got up first time." Daisy's chest expanded proudly.

"Good work. Now, could you carry the sunscreen back to the house? I'll take the towels. I think Daddy's going to have to carry Jenna. She fell asleep in the boat."

"Sure." Daisy skipped ahead with Andie and Drew, who was carrying a sleeping Angel in his arms.

"Too much excitement for the little ones, I guess," Kirk said, plucking Jenna from the bottom of the boat.

"We can put them down on my bed," Grady suggested. "Then let's organize something to eat. I'm starved, and I think Claire has something decadent in that container of hers."

At the mention of food, Andie and Daisy looked back from where they were walking with Drew. Both spotted the plastic container in their mother's hands and called out simultaneously, "Triple Temptation Cookies?"

Claire just smiled and picked up the box.

Following behind Grady and Kirk, along the deck that led to the back patio door, she couldn't help but visually compare the two men. They were close in height, but so different in character and in build. Grady was larger—broader across the shoulders and rugged in form—whereas Kirk's muscles were more sharply defined, his hips slimmer, his body movements almost graceful.

Two such different men. One dark, one fair; one a craftsman, the other a businessman.

If she had it all to do over again, if the choice rested entirely in her hands, which would she want to marry?

Kirk had said she couldn't answer the question. And he was right.

But not because the answer was so difficult. Because the question was wrong. Second-guessing past choices was a fool's game. The thought hit her a few minutes later, once the younger children were tucked under covers and Grady had found everyone something to drink. She was sitting at the patio table across from Kirk, who was checking Andie carefully for signs of sunburn.

"Seems okay, kiddo," he said. "Guess that sun lotion really was waterproof like it said."

Andie slid onto Kirk's knee, wrapping an arm around his neck. With their heads so close together, Claire could see a resemblance in the shape of their chins and the deep set of their eyes. Andie was a doll, and her husband was gorgeous. With his now-bronzed skin and sun-bleached hair, he reminded her of how he'd looked that first summer they'd gone out.

He'd been playing baseball, and she'd attended all his games to cheer him on. He'd been an awesome shortstop, and a fabulous sight in his uniform. Claire recollected one game in particular, when she'd sat behind two young women who spent the whole game listing Kirk's obvious physical charms and screaming every time he made a good play. After the game, their whispers had become hushed when he headed their way, then their mouths had dropped open to see him walk up to Claire and throw his arms around her.

She'd felt so proud of him then, and proud of herself, too—that he'd chosen her as his girl. Claire smiled, remembering, then suddenly felt more somber. When had she lost the feeling that she was the chosen one? That for Kirk the sun rose and fell around her and the things she said and did?

"Okay, Claire," Grady said, breaking into her

thoughts. "Enough with the mystery. Show us the goods."

"Aw, it's nothing," Claire said, removing the lid slowly. "Just a double batch of those cookies nobody ever seems to like very much."

Three heads crashed as they bent in simultaneously.

"Ow!" Daisy complained. But a cheer followed immediately. "Yeah! Triple Temptation Cookies!"

They passed the box around, once, twice and again, until the cookies were almost all gone. Made with a chocolate-drop cookie base and generous scoops of semisweet chocolate chips, white-chocolate chips and chopped almonds, they were a triple-chocolate delight and a favorite of adults and kids alike.

A fitting "end of the season" contribution to her "Cottage Cooking" column? Claire shied from the thought, shocked to realize how quickly the summer had passed.

She'd planned on having her marriage problems sorted out before the kids were back in school. But after two months of counseling, talking, arguing and discussing, she felt they were no further ahead than when they'd started. She cast a look at Kirk, wondering if he felt equally discouraged.

KIRK BIT INTO THE COOKIE his wife had baked, barely tasting the rich, fudgey flavor. He was captivated by the picture Claire made, with her flaxen hair mussed from the wind and her skin flushed from a day in the heat. She'd taken off her sunglasses in the shade of the awning over Grady's deck, and the blue of her eyes appeared even more intense than usual.

You'd think that after all these years he'd be accustomed to her beauty. True, weeks could go by without him really noticing her. But then there would be a moment when the sun hit her a certain way or she paused with her head tilted at just the right angle.

And *wham,* it would hit him, just like the very first time he'd met her—at the firm's Christmas party. She was working at the hotel and the moment she stepped into the ballroom—to make sure the event was proceeding as planned—the world had stopped rotating, he'd ceased breathing, the lights had dimmed. Except for one hot spotlight trained directly on her face. The wonder girl who could have brought him to his knees on the strength of her warm, husky laugh alone.

From that first moment, he'd determined to meet her, to date her, to marry her. He'd never felt a moment's doubt that she was the woman for him, and the more he'd gotten to know her, the more certain he'd grown in his feelings.

This was the woman he wanted.

Had she ever felt that way about him? Had she ever felt anything even close to it? Watching her now, Kirk realized his wife was as much of an enigma to him as ever.

"Want another cookie, Daddy?" Andie held the box in front of him. "It's the very last one."

"That's generous of you. Thanks, kiddo." He took the cookie, broke it in half and offered the larger piece to his daughter.

Daisy, her delicate mouth now edged in chocolate, looked at the empty box and sighed. "Are there any more at home?"

"Afraid not, hon." Claire lifted her onto her lap, and Daisy snuggled her head against her mother's shoulder.

They're a picture, those two. Same coloring, same vivid blue eyes. He wanted to reach for the camera, which he'd brought with him on the boat, but he was so comfortable with Andie sprawled against him.

"Well, now that we've had dessert, how about a main course?" Grady asked. "I know the boys will be home soon, starving as usual. Burgers okay with everyone?"

"We should be going," Claire protested.

"Don't you dare." Grady placed a hand against her empty shoulder, the one without Daisy snuggled into it, to force her back in the chair. "Jenna's sound asleep, and besides, it's my turn to entertain.

Why does everyone assume that since Beth left I'm not capable of scraping a meal together? Who do you think did most of the cooking when she lived here, anyway?''

"It must have been you," Drew said. "Or those boys would never have grown as tall as they are. Remember that sauce Bess made for Claire's Christmas pudding a few years ago?''

Drew pushed his chair back. "I'll give you a hand, Grady. Let's call Mallory and ask her to bring a tub of coleslaw from Marg's on her way home from work.''

"I'll help, too," Claire volunteered, but Grady stuck his head out the door to refuse her offer.

"You can't cook. You're a living lounge chair." His gaze dropped to Daisy, whose eyelids were drooping. "Relax for a change and let someone else take care of the grub.''

Kirk had been about to volunteer, as well, but Andie was falling asleep against him. "These kids aren't so much hungry as exhausted.''

Claire nodded. She was gazing at Daisy's face, and her dreamy expression reminded him of the way she looked when she was nursing an infant.

Kirk choked up, wondering if he would have the privilege of watching while she nursed this new baby. Right now the odds weren't good.

He'd really hoped counseling would be the answer, but as far as he could tell they hadn't made much progress. His tirade last night hadn't helped. Why had he lost his cool that way? He hadn't seriously thought there was anything going on between Grady and Claire.

But he *was* jealous. Not just of the close friendship or the high regard that Claire had for Grady, but of the time Grady had always been able to spend with his family.

Did Claire think he *wanted* to miss dinners with the family, the children's little performances, time together on the weekend? Long office hours, a forty-five-minute commute, extensive travel demands—these were the realities of the job he had chosen. And Kirk loved his job.

But he also loved his wife.

If only she could love him back. For the man he was, not the husband and father she wanted him to be.

Was that asking too much?

"There's something we need to talk about."

From Claire's tone of voice, it wasn't anything good. Feeling a sudden panic, Kirk checked to make sure Andie was sleeping, before asking, "What is it?"

"I got the results from that blood test I took in Barrie."

Kirk's thoughts shifted from the relationship between him and Claire to their unborn child. "And?"

"The alpha-something or other levels were a little high. The doctor is recommending I have an amniocentesis so they can test the baby's cells in the amniotic fluid."

Kirk was at a loss for a moment. "But—" He paused, thinking things through. "What will they be checking for?"

Claire sighed. "Well, one of their concerns is neural tube defects."

"You mean like spina bifida?"

She nodded. "It's a possibility. Of course, if they do the amnio, they'll test for other things, too. Like Down's syndrome."

Kirk sucked in a deep breath.

"This test is just a precaution. Chances are the baby is fine."

"Of course she is." But then, why had the blood test come back abnormal? Kirk felt a rising panic; he knew women over age thirty-five were at increased risk for fetal anomalies.

He tried not to let the worry sound in his voice. "How soon can you have the amnio?"

"I've got an appointment booked for Monday morning. I wasn't sure if I was going to keep it. But I guess I should, huh?"

"I think so, Claire. Even just for the peace of mind."

"The amnio has risks, too, you know." Claire

pushed her hair back from her forehead. "There's a one in two hundred possibility of miscarriage."

Damn. Those odds weren't as small as he'd like. However, they were talking about serious defects here. "I don't know, Claire. What do *you* think?"

"I'm sure the baby is fine. Still…"

"Maybe we ought to be certain."

"Yes." She sighed. "I guess I'll keep that appointment."

"Monday morning, right? I'll call in late to the office and come with you."

THE AMNIOCENTESIS WASN'T so much painful as it was uncomfortable. Claire had to drink eight glasses of water beforehand, which put a real strain on her bladder. First, the doctor located the baby's position by ultrasound, then she swabbed Claire's belly with sepia-colored antiseptic.

"To prevent infection," she explained, taking out a hypodermic needle that looked frighteningly long.

Claire squeezed Kirk's fingers and forced her gaze away from the needle.

"You'll feel a pinprick as the needle goes in," the doctor told her, "then pressure as we draw out a couple of tablespoons of amniotic fluid. Hopefully, we'll gather some of the baby's shed skin cells with the fluid."

Claire closed her eyes and squeezed Kirk's hand tighter.

He bent low and kissed the top of her head. "You're being very brave."

As she felt the needle jab her skin, Claire focused on the baby. *You're going to be okay. Don't start doing cartwheels now, whatever you do.* The pressing deep inside her was like nothing she'd ever experienced. Then it was over, and the doctor was reminding her of things to watch out for.

"Leakage from the vagina, abdominal cramps or fever. If you have any of these symptoms, call us immediately."

"We will," Kirk promised. He appeared calm and confident in his suit and tie, but behind his tan, his skin was almost as pale as his starched white shirt. "Are you okay, Claire?"

She nodded, feeling unaccountably teary. They had to wait three to four weeks for the results of this test. An interminable period of time. Not that she was going to worry. *Her baby was okay. She just knew it.*

CHAPTER TWENTY-ONE

CLAIRE FELT as if she'd blinked twice and the summer had gone. Fruit stands were loaded with fresh, locally grown corn, apples, potatoes and squash; stores everywhere offered back-to-school specials; dresses that had fallen to her girls' knees in June were now too short.

The September long weekend was hot and glorious. It seemed a travesty to pack up and return to the city. Kirk came up to help her organize belongings, clean out the fridge, load up the van.

"I don't want to go to the city," Daisy complained, hanging on to the tire swing Saturday after lunch.

Claire sympathized. She wasn't ready to go home yet, either. Her life was still a shambles; she had no clear idea about the right thing to do. And yet, the time had arrived to make a decision. Starting tonight, she and Kirk would be living under the same roof seven days a week. Given the reluctant truce they'd reached since Kirk's blowup about Grady, she wasn't sure either of them could bear the strain.

"We'll be back for Thanksgiving," Kirk said as he passed with two of the suitcases.

But would they?

Claire felt hot just watching him work. She'd changed into her denim jumper after lunch dishes were done, and already her legs were sticky under the long fabric. She was exhausted, and not anticipating the three-hour drive with much enthusiasm.

"Come on, Daisy. Get into the van, please." Jenna was already buckled into the back seat of the Volvo, and Andie had claimed the front seat next to her dad.

"I want to ride with Daddy."

"But *I'm* going with Daddy," Andie objected.

"There's room for all three of you," Kirk pointed out.

"I don't care." Andie crossed her arms and leaned against the door. "I'm not riding with *her*."

Daisy's face was red as she gave in quietly and climbed into the van.

Claire tamped down an impulse to scream at Andie and looked mutely, instead, at Kirk. He shook his head, not having to speak for her to know what he was thinking. *What should we do?*

Claire was too tired to force a confrontation. With a sigh she climbed into the driver's seat, while Kirk went back inside for the final load. He came out carrying a box of perishable food.

"That's the last of it." Kirk shut the back door

to the van firmly, then walked around the driver's side. He stuck a hand in the open window and ruffled Daisy's hair. "Are you sure you don't want to come in the car? Andie doesn't set the rules around here, you know."

Daisy shook her head, her bottom lip full, her eyes shiny with tears. "I'm going with Mommy."

Claire glanced back at the cottage, all locked up, blinds pulled over the windows. Once again she acknowledged that she wasn't ready to leave. But she had no choice. Her kids had to go to school. Once again, too, she acknowledged that she had to start living with her husband again. That, or get up the courage to tell him to leave.

Which was it to be?

Stomach burning, she secured her seat belt, slipped on her sunglasses.

"Ready?" Kirk asked.

She nodded, then twisted the key. As she drove off without looking back, the knowledge that they'd return for Thanksgiving provided cold comfort. Thanksgiving was almost two months away. And a lot could happen in two months.

THEY MADE GOOD TIME on the trip, and Claire pulled the van into the garage just before four o'clock, Kirk's Volvo right behind her. She got out and stretched, easing the kinks from her shoulders and back.

"Excuse me, Mom." Andie tried to push past in the restricted space of the garage.

"Let me shut my door. What's the rush?"

"I want to put up that postcard Mallory and Drew sent me from the Gatineau Hills. And I want to see all my stuffed animals again."

Claire opened the passenger door for Daisy, then went round the back, where Kirk was already removing luggage.

"I'll do the unloading," he said. "And I was thinking we should order in pizza for dinner tonight. Sound okay?"

"Good idea." They'd have enough work to do getting unpacked and settled without preparing a meal, as well.

"You go inside and rest for a minute," Kirk said, lugging two suitcases and Daisy's backpack. "It's a long drive in the hot sun."

Claire shepherded in the younger girls, then fixed them a small snack before collapsing on the sofa. Andie was still in her room, and frankly, Claire hoped she would stay there awhile. That crack about not driving with Daisy hadn't been the first mean thing Andie had said to her younger sister today, and Claire had just about had it.

Kirk dumped the suitcases of dirty clothes in the laundry room and placed the perishables in the fridge. By then, Claire was refreshed enough to supervise baths for the children, while Kirk phoned in their pizza order.

"Bath time," she said, shooing them up the stairs.

"But I don't want one," Daisy grumbled.

"Pretend it's the lake," Claire suggested.

"Then I want to wear my bathing suit."

"Will we need to wear life jackets?" Jenna wondered.

Claire rolled her eyes. "What have I started?"

"Don't worry." Kirk was coming up the stairs behind her. "I can handle this. You go have a bath of your own."

"Are you sure?" At Kirk's nod, she left them to it and headed for the master bathroom. As she passed Andie's room, she noticed her daughter reading as usual.

"You need to have a bath, too, Andie."

"I'm not a baby. I'll have a shower when they're done."

"Fine." Claire retreated to the master suite and turned on the water in her sunken tub and added a handful of bath salts. A good long soak was the one thing she missed when she went to the cottage for the summer, since they had only the one shower.

The denim jumper came off in one long tug; her T-shirt and underwear followed quickly. She searched one of the bags Kirk had brought up earlier and found her latest mystery novel. Ready at last, she stepped down into the tub.

Scented water engulfed her naked body, and she sighed with the physical pleasure of warmth and the tang of lavender. She stretched out her legs and cupped her hands over her mounded tummy.

For two chapters, she was lost to the world. The next thing she knew, the doorbell was ringing and the water felt lukewarm.

"Pizza! Pizza!" Jenna's voice reverberated throughout the house.

Claire wrapped herself in a terry robe, then hurried downstairs to set plates around the table and pour glasses of milk. Kirk placed the cardboard pizza boxes in the center of the table, his wet hair clinging to his head. When had he found time to take a shower?

"Two pieces, please," Daisy said. "I'm starving."

Kirk opened the box and the smell of tomato sauce and warm bread had everyone leaning forward.

Everyone except Andie.

"I don't like that kind."

"There's plain cheese and tomato," Kirk pointed out.

"I don't want that, either."

Claire sighed and hoped the girls would go to

sleep after dinner. She was so tired she would go to bed right after them.

Which would conveniently finesse the bedroom issue. Claire had no idea whether Kirk expected to sleep in the same bed as her now that they were home. She knew she ought to have broached the topic with him earlier; she couldn't ask him to sleep on the couch seven days a week. But what alternatives did they have? She couldn't imagine sleeping a wink if he was beside her.

"Mom, tell Daisy to eat with her mouth closed," Andie complained.

Daisy seemed startled. "I am."

"No, you're not. You're making too much noise, and you're disgusting to watch."

Daisy started to cry and Claire looked at Andie, at a loss to understand these recent outbursts. "Don't talk to your sister that way, Andie."

"Why not? I hate her! She's stupid and ugly and I wish she'd never been born!" Andie jumped up from her chair and ran for her room. Daisy started crying all the harder.

"Oh, my Lord." Claire pushed a hand through her damp hair and wondered if they could install a lock on the *outside* of Andie's door. At his end of the table, Kirk appeared as fed up as she felt.

"I can't believe Andie would talk that way."

Claire shook her head, then reached over to

Daisy. "Don't cry, hon. Your sister didn't mean those things she said."

The legs of Kirk's chair scraped against the floor. "I'm going to speak with her."

Claire nodded, trying to tamp down the anger she couldn't help but feel toward her eldest daughter. The attack on Daisy had been completely unprovoked, at least as far as she could tell.

Daisy had pushed her plate aside, and now she turned to her mother. "Why doesn't Andie like me anymore?"

The question wrenched Claire's heart. "Your sister *loves* you, Daisy. She's just feeling unhappy, and…"

And taking it out on her younger sister. But why? Was she worried about school starting again? She'd managed to complete the math workbook this summer without any difficulty. Which made Claire wonder all the more about those poor grades. Andie could handle the work. Last year, she'd just chosen not to.

Claire picked up Daisy and pulled her onto her lap. Or what was left of it.

"I don't think she does like me." Daisy pushed her face into Claire's shoulder. "She never wants to play anymore. All she does is read and complain about how noisy I am."

Claire hugged her tighter, thankful that at least Jenna wasn't letting the scene upset her. She'd finished her first slice of pizza, having eaten down to the hard edge of the crust. Now she looked at Claire to see if it was okay for her to have seconds.

Claire settled Daisy back in her chair, then placed a fresh slice on both Daisy's and Jenna's plates. "Try to eat a little more, hon," she said to Daisy. "And don't worry about your sister. She'll come around. I'm sure."

Once Daisy was calm, Claire left the two girls at the table and followed the sound of Andie's sobs up the stairs. Kirk had taken Andie into their bedroom. Looking into Andie's room and seeing the stuffed animals and the postcards their eldest had thrown around in a rage, Claire understood why. She returned to the door of the master suite, pausing at the sound of her husband's voice.

"Sh, sweetie, sh," Kirk was saying between Andie's sobs. "Sh, sweetie."

Peering into the room, Claire saw him holding Andie against his chest, stroking her hair with one hand. Gradually, Andie's cries subsided.

"You must be feeling awful inside to have said those things to your sister. What's wrong, Andie?"

The comment was astute, and as Andie began sobbing again, Claire put a hand to her forehead. The poor kid. She sounded as if her heart was breaking.

Oh, Andie. Andie.

Why hadn't she herself been as insightful as

Kirk? Of course Andie had to be hurting to have said those things. Only, why was Andie so unhappy? Claire had tried hard to give her extra attention this summer.

"Daddy, are you and Mom going to get a divorce?"

Claire covered her mouth and sank to the carpet. Kirk was quiet for several moments before he spoke.

"Why do you ask that?"

"Because my friend Erin's parents got a divorce. And she gave me a list of things to watch out for. And, Daddy—every one of them is happening to you and Mom—except for the yelling."

"Oh, my Lord, Andie. When did Erin give you this list?"

"The week after Christmas."

Which was when her marks had begun to drop, and her interest in friends had declined. All this time Claire had thought Andie was having a problem with her friends, but the problem was her parents.

"You were on a business trip," Andie continued, "and Mom said I could have Erin for a sleepover. We talked all night. She said that one of the signs is when the dad is hardly ever home."

"But, Andie, I've always taken business trips."

"Not as many as this year. You sent me seven

postcards. Last year I only got three. Daddy, I feel so sick whenever you go away.''

Claire bit her lip, remembering Andie's constant, anxious queries about her father. *When is Daddy coming?* They'd tried so hard to protect the children from their troubles. But they'd forgotten Andie was growing up....

''I know you slept on the couch every night at the cottage, Daddy. That was another sign.''

''Oh, sweetheart.''

Claire could hear the rustle of cloth and assumed Kirk was giving Andie another hug. She wanted to rush in and hug her daughter, too, but the interruption might stop Andie from talking, and she'd been bottling all this inside for far too long already.

''Marriages are very private things,'' Kirk began. ''But you've got to trust your mom and me to do the best we can. I know it's hard, but you know we'll always look after you and love you. Right?''

Andie sniffled. ''But, Daddy. I want us to all stay together.''

''We're together now, aren't we?''

''Yes, but—''

''Never mind Erin's list, okay? Let me tell you something that I know is true.''

''What?''

''Those things on that list also happen to dads and moms who stay together.''

"They do?"

"Ask any couple."

"Even Mallory and Drew?"

Kirk laughed. "Yes. Even them."

"But Grady and Bess got divorced, Daddy. It *does* happen."

Claire could hear Kirk's sigh as clearly as if he were right beside her.

"Yes. You're right," he replied. "Sometimes divorce *does* happen."

Claire eased herself back up to her feet and went downstairs. She'd failed her eldest daughter. How could she have been so insensitive? For the past six months Andie had been worrying about the family falling apart so much that she'd lost interest in her schoolwork and her friends. It was so obvious now.

Claire went through the motions of cleaning up from dinner, then put the younger girls to bed. Fortunately, they were both exhausted, so it didn't take much effort. When they were asleep, she finally dared to go back upstairs. She found Andie curled up in her father's arms, both Andie and Kirk asleep on the king-size bed in the master bedroom.

Claire stood watching them for a long time, all too aware that a solution to the trouble in their family wasn't going to drop out of the sky like a lucky lotto ticket and quickly fix their problems.

She reached a hand to Andie's forehead to brush

back a strand of hair and in that moment felt the absolute simplicity of the solution. It could come from her and it could come from Kirk. And all it would take to make it work was a firm commitment.

What if, she wondered with an almost dizzying perception of how marriage could be, *what if she and Kirk loved each other with the same boundless, unconditional love they showered on their children?* What if she could make Kirk feel he was "the one and only"? If he could make her feel she was the most precious woman on earth?

Claire looked down on her husband's face, seeing a vulnerability that wasn't visible when he was awake. She thought of the boy she'd married—the handsome, blond baseball champ; the keen young stockbroker with more plans than clients, more energy than cash. Kirk's specialty was investments. Well, was there any greater than the one they'd made in each other?

"I love you." As she murmured the words Claire touched his cheek lightly, then Andie's. Her family. Her heart ached with the need to hold them close, to protect them.

"Come here." Kirk whispered the words, extending his one free arm.

"I didn't know you were awake."

"I'm not. Just dreaming I'm in this wonderful

place where I'm hugging my wife and my daughter so tightly I'll never lose either of them.''

Kirk's hand found hers, and he pulled her down. ''Come, Claire....''

He tucked her in next to him, her face on his chest, his arm circling her shoulder. She could smell the soap he'd used in the shower, the fabric softener on his clean T-shirt. She curled her legs up over his and felt her foot against Andie's leg. Her daughter sighed and snuggled in closer to her dad.

''I love you, Claire. I love you.'' The words settled like a warm blanket around her heart. She put a hand to her husband's cheek and allowed her eyes to relax and close.

''I love you, too.''

She hadn't felt this safe in a long time.

IN THE MIDDLE OF THE NIGHT, Claire felt something on her cheek. She reached to smooth it away, thinking it was a strand of her hair. But it wasn't. It was a hand.

Claire opened her eyes and saw Andie, still lying next to Kirk, watching her. She reached up, squeezed Andie's hand and smiled.

''Mommy.''

''I'm here, honey.''

Andie sighed, closed her eyes, and fell back asleep.

SOMETIME IN THE NIGHT Jenna and Daisy must have had a nightmare. Or maybe they'd just woken up and felt strange not being at the cottage. At any rate, when morning came Kirk saw that Daisy was lying next to Claire, while Jenna was partly on top of him.

"Daddy?" Jenna rolled a little so their faces were practically touching. "I feel funny."

"Funny in what way?"

"My tooth." Jenna wiggled it with her tongue, causing the skin under her bottom lip to bulge. "Check it, Daddy."

Obligingly, Kirk dislodged his hand from under Andie's shoulders, and reached in to take a tug. "Oh."

"What is it, Daddy?" Jenna asked, unaware that she now had a small gap in her bottom front teeth.

"Guess what I found." He put the tooth in her hand.

"My tooth! I lost my tooth!" Jenna bounded up and down on his chest. "Daisy, I lost a tooth, too!"

"Let me see." Daisy leaned over Claire to get a better look.

"First Mommy sees."

Claire was just waking, her eyelids heavy as she brushed her hair back from her forehead to peer at the treasure. "Wow, hon—your first tooth!"

"Kind of nice, isn't it?" Kirk murmured in Claire's ear. "Having them all in bed with us."

It was the *us* part that was the best. He remembered Claire lying down with him and Andie earlier. That she'd fallen asleep, stayed the night, had to be a good sign.

"A little crowded. But very nice." Claire smiled at him with drowsy warmth. "Good thing we have a king-size bed."

Kirk shifted his long legs to make room for Jenna and Daisy, who were now tumbling at the foot of the bed, tickling each other and giggling. While Andie still slept....

"It's only going to get more crowded. Soon we'll be six."

Kirk focused on his wife, wondering if she'd considered the import of the words she'd just spoken.

He thought probably she had, judging by the way she was looking at him right now, her eyes so full of...

"I probably don't tell you this enough, Kirk, but I think you're a fantastic success. I've always been proud to be your wife."

Love. Her look was so full of love, and it was directed at *him*.

"I want to be a good husband and father, Claire."

"You are."

"I think I could be better." This summer he'd taken off *every* weekend. And it hadn't been that hard. Surely, if he was organized and determined and maybe sacrificed just a little of his ambition at work...

She kissed him then, and he pulled her close, waking Andie with the movement. She groaned, then turned over, finally opening her eyes.

"We're all in the same bed!" Andie looked amazed, and happier than Kirk could remember.

Claire reached out to her daughter in the same instant that he did. "You know," she said. "I want to gather you all in the world's biggest, tightest hug. Come here, Jenna and Daisy."

They collapsed in a pile, together, and Kirk saw the tear, just before it fell off Claire's cheek onto the pillow. He rubbed her skin with his finger, then kissed the spot gently. He felt the same bittersweet happiness that he knew she was experiencing. How close they'd come to losing all this.

"Andie? How about fixing your sisters some breakfast so your mother and I can get a few more minutes' sleep?"

"Daddy, I'm tired," Andie moaned. Then quickly she sat up. "You and Mom are going to sleep *together,* right?"

"That's right."

"Okay. Come on, kids. I'll toast you some frozen waffles. I saw them in the freezer last night."

"Yay! Frozen waffles!" Jenna and Daisy scooted out of bed.

Andie hung back at the door. "Okay, you guys. You can go ahead and *sleep* now." She smiled at them, then shut the door firmly behind her.

Claire looked at Kirk. "You don't think she suspects…"

"Of course she does." Kirk slid his hand inside her robe and pulled her to him tightly. "We're the ones who explained it to her, remember?"

"Yes, but..." She closed her eyes in pleasure as he began massaging her shoulder.

"Have I told you yet this morning how much I love you?" he asked. "I missed you and the girls so much this summer. But it did give me time to think things over. I'll do whatever it takes to earn your trust again. Claire, it may help you to know that Janice has left the firm."

"Oh?" His wife went still. "Because of you?"

He nodded. "I didn't ask her to leave, but I was glad when she came to the decision herself."

Claire remained stiff, and for a moment he felt a hint of panic. He shouldn't have mentioned the name of the woman who'd almost come between them.

"Is it because you still care...?"

"God, no." He covered her mouth with a kiss. "I just thought it would make it easier for you if she wasn't around. Not to have to wonder..."

"Yes. It probably will. But I do trust you, Kirk."

"Claire, those words mean so much to me. I'm not going to let you down again."

"I know." She ran her hand lovingly down the side of his face. "And for the record, there's something you need to be sure of."

"Yeah?" He caught her hand and pressed her fingers to his lips.

"You're the man I love, the only man I'd ever choose to marry."

Kirk believed her. There was a light in her eyes as she looked at him that he couldn't remember seeing before. Or maybe it had been there once, in the beginning...

"Kirk, I know I've held back too much for too long. I'm not going to do that anymore."

Inside her robe, his hand followed the curve of her back, down over her bottom, then up the front of her thigh.

The small moan she gave was encouraging. He continued the caress, up to the mound of her belly.

"I'm so excited about this baby, Claire." He ignored a twinge of anxiety about the amnio test results, due any day. "Can you believe we're going to have a fourth child?"

"Well, that's what happens, you know." She slipped her hand down the elastic waistband of his sweatpants, drawing in her breath at finding him hard and ready.

"Show me again how we did it," he urged.

And she did.

CHAPTER TWENTY-TWO

Cottage Cooking, by Claire Ridgeway
The important thing about cooking for the holidays is making it fun. If you have to spend the day in the kitchen—and you do—arrange for everyone else to be in there with you. Crank up your favorite music. Pour yourself a glass of something bubbly and light. Get the kids shelling the nuts while your hubby chops veggies. You're the boss. Let *them* get their hands dirty. You've got a manicure to protect.

Sound like a pipe dream? Well, it probably is, unless you've got cable TV hooked up where hubby can see it from the sink, and you're prepared to bribe your children with lots of treats that will spoil their appetite for dinner.

If not, fall on the backup plan, which is to make this dressing a few days ahead of time. Serve it with fresh roasted turkey and I guarantee it will be a hit. Every year my friends beg me for the recipe. This year they're getting it: "Claire's Hazelnut Dressing with Cranberries and Brandy"...

"I CAN'T BELIEVE the secret is finally out." Mallory held up the clipping from the previous week's issue of the *Gazette*. "Are you sure you didn't leave something out? Some crucial ingredient so no matter how many people try the recipe it'll never be as good as yours?"

"You are a suspicious person, do you know that?" Claire walked out from behind the kitchen sink, only it felt more like waddling. At over seven months she was bigger than she'd been for any of her other children at this stage. Kirk pulled out her chair, then jogged to the other end of their massive pine table.

There were twenty-one of them for Thanksgiving this year, and she still couldn't believe they'd managed to fit around one table. One very long table, thanks to a little quick construction work on Grady's part.

Claire lifted her glass of nonalcoholic wine and looked around at everyone. "Toasts?" She knew what she would drink to, later when just she and Kirk were on their own. To reconciliations and families and making the word *commitment* really mean something.

Now Grady had something to say. He was standing, holding his glass in one hand and Terese's hand in the other. ''I'm feeling pretty good today, and not just because we're all together for another year. She finally said yes, guys. Terese has agreed to marry me!'' Grady raised his glass high, and a cheer broke out around the table.

Claire smiled, feeling true happiness for her friend and his future bride. She wasn't so conceited as to think her talk with Terese had precipitated the young woman's change of heart, but she did hope it had helped just a little. From the way Terese had smiled at her when she'd walked into the cottage with Grady, Claire was inclined to think that it had.

At the other end of the table, she saw that Kirk shared her pleasure at Grady's announcement and, more important, that no trace of the old jealousy was left between them.

Next Patricia Conroy got up to toast Buddy's first year of semiretirement, then Drew made a toast to old friends. Finally, Kirk rose, his eyes on Claire as he lifted his glass.

''Claire and I got the results from the amniocentesis a few weeks ago. We waited until we were all together to let you know that the baby is fine—'' he paused for cheers, then continued ''—and to announce that we're expecting a boy.'' He blinked rapidly, then shrugged. ''And just as we were getting kind of good at girls, too.''

Poor Kirk had been in such shock when they'd

first heard the news. He'd kept asking if there could be some mistake. Somehow they'd both expected another girl. But it seemed fitting they were stepping out of the groove, since they'd changed so many things in their life together. Small things—like the two of them going out every Friday night, and Kirk reserving Sundays for family time—but important things. Their renewed love and commitment, Claire was certain, would see them through the challenges that lay ahead.

After dinner, and a slice of Mallory's pumpkin pie for dessert, each of Claire's girls came up to their mother with questions about the baby.

"Does this mean I'm going to have a brother?" Jenna asked.

"Yes, it does."

"Will I have to share my room with a boy?" Daisy asked.

"Would you rather share with Jenna?"

"Oh, yes."

"Then that's what we'll do."

Andie wondered if you could cuddle a boy baby as much as a girl.

"Definitely. Little boys need lots of loving, just like little girls."

As Grady's sons cleared the table and Terese filled the sink with water to do the dishes, Kirk pulled Claire onto his lap. "No cleanup duties for you, chef. You need to take a break."

Claire wasn't about to argue. Her feet were killing her. She slipped off her shoes, and Kirk reached down to give her a quick massage.

Claire closed her eyes and purred. "Have I told you lately how wonderful you are?" All around she heard the sounds of her family and friends. The girls were playing Twister on the old pine floor, and most of the adults were helping in the kitchen, laughing and joking as usual.

"Excuse me, you lovebirds," Grady said, walking past them. "I'm going to light a fire. It's getting a little chilly."

"Speak for yourself," Kirk said, nuzzling his face against Claire's neck.

Once the fire was going, Kirk whispered into her ear, "You know, I think we could slip out for half an hour and not even be missed."

Claire propped herself up on her elbows. "What are you thinking?"

Kirk nodded out the window. Dusk had settled; it was almost dark. "Could be a nice evening for a canoe ride."

"A canoe ride?" Claire laughed, knowing where this was leading. She glanced around the room. It was true; everyone was busy. No one was even looking their way. "Okay."

"Grab a coat on the way out," Kirk said. "I'll get a blanket. Meet you at the pier."

Feeling deliciously naughty, Claire nonchalantly

headed for the door, grabbing at her fleece jacket, which hung from the wall. Making love in a canoe had been a challenge at the age of twenty-four. Now she was twelve years older and almost seven and a half months pregnant. The two of them had to be crazy.

Just as she was about to slip out the door, she noticed Mallory standing at the counter, watching her every move.

"Sh." Claire put her finger to her mouth.

Mallory gave a sly smile. "Watch out for owls."

Claire shut the door, trying not to laugh. Sometimes your friends could know you too well.

Claire's
Cranberry, Hazelnut, Brandy Dressing

Soften $1/3$ cup dried cranberries in $1/4$ cup orange brandy for one hour.

Sauté 1 chopped onion and $1/2$ cup chopped celery in 3 tablespoons butter.

Combine onion mixture, cranberries and brandy and the following:

4 cups dried whole-wheat bread cubes
$1/2$ cup chopped hazelnuts
zest from 1 orange
1 teaspoon poultry seasoning
1 teaspoon salt
$1/8$ teaspoon pepper

Stuff dressing in turkey cavity. Bake as usual.

HARLEQUIN®
SUPERROMANCE®

Pregnant and alone—
these stories follow women
from the heartache of
betrayal to finding true love
and starting a family.

THE FOURTH CHILD by **C.J. Carmichael**.
When Claire's marriage is in trouble, she tries to
save it—although she's not sure she can forgive her
husband's betrayal.
On sale May 2000.

AND BABY MAKES SIX by **Linda Markowiak**.
Jenny suddenly finds herself jobless and pregnant by
a man who doesn't want their child.
On sale June 2000.

MOM'S THE WORD by **Roz Denny Fox**.
After her feckless husband steals her inheritance and
leaves town with another woman, Hayley discovers she's
pregnant.
On sale July 2000.

Available wherever Harlequin books are sold.

HARLEQUIN®
Makes any time special ™

Visit us at www.eHarlequin.com   HSR9ML01

Looking For More Romance?

Visit Romance.net

Look us up on-line at: http://www.romance.net

Check in daily for these and other exciting features:

Hot off the press

View all current titles, and purchase them on-line.

What do the stars have in store for you?

Horoscope

Hot deals

Exclusive offers available only at Romance.net

Plus, don't miss our interactive quizzes, contests and bonus gifts.

Your Romantic Books—find them at

www.eHarlequin.com

Visit the *Author's Alcove*

➤ Find the most complete information anywhere on your favorite author.

➤ Try your hand in the Writing Round Robin— contribute a chapter to an online book in the making.

Enter the *Reading Room*

➤ Experience an interactive novel—help determine the fate of a story being created now by one of your favorite authors.

➤ Join one of our reading groups and discuss your favorite book.

Drop into *Shop eHarlequin*

➤ Find the latest releases—read an excerpt or write a review for this month's Harlequin top sellers.

➤ Try out our amazing search feature—tell us your favorite theme, setting or time period and we'll find a book that's perfect for you.

All this and more available at

www.eHarlequin.com
on Women.com Networks